W9-AFQ-743

4 books in 1!

#1

-- The Un-Friendship Bracelet --

#2

-- Making the Band --

#3

-- Tie-Dye Disaster --

#4

-- Dream Machine --

By Martha Maker Illustrated by Xindi Yan

LITTLE SIMON
New York London Toronto Sydney New Delhi

This book is a work of fiction. Any references to historical events, real people, or real places are used fictitiously. Other names, characters, places, and events are products of the author's imagination, and any resemblance to actual events or places or persons, living or dead, is entirely coincidental.

LITTLE SIMON
An imprint of Simon & Schuster Children's Publishing Division
1230 Avenue of the Americas, New York, New York 10020
This Little Simon bind-up edition May 2019

For information about special discounts for bulk purchases, please contact Simon & Schuster Special Sales at 1-866-506-1949 or business@simonandschuster.com. The Simon & Schuster Speakers Bureau can bring authors to your live event. For more information or to book an event contact the Simon & Schuster Speakers Bureau at 1-866-248-3049 or visit our website at www.simonspeakers.com.
Designed by Laura Roode
Manufactured in the United States of America 0419 FFG
2 4 6 8 10 9 7 5 3 1
ISBN 978-1-5344-5634-1
ISBN 978-1-5344-0909-5 (*The Un-Friendship Bracelet* eBook)
ISBN 978-1-5344-0912-5 (*Making the Band* eBook)
ISBN 978-1-5344-1729-8 (*Tie-Dye Disaster* eBook)
ISBN 978-1-5344-1732-8 (*Dream Machine* eBook)

CONTENTS

The Un-Friendship Bracelet

CONTENTS

CHAPTER
1
P.E

Meet MAD-ILY

"Emily! I missed you so much!"

Maddie Wilson ran across the classroom and swept Emily Adams into a huge hug. Emily had only been away at her grandparents' house for the weekend, but for best friends who called themselves "MAD-ILY," two days could feel like forever.

"You too!" Emily said. She pulled back and looked Maddie up and down. "Did you get new . . . everything?" she asked.

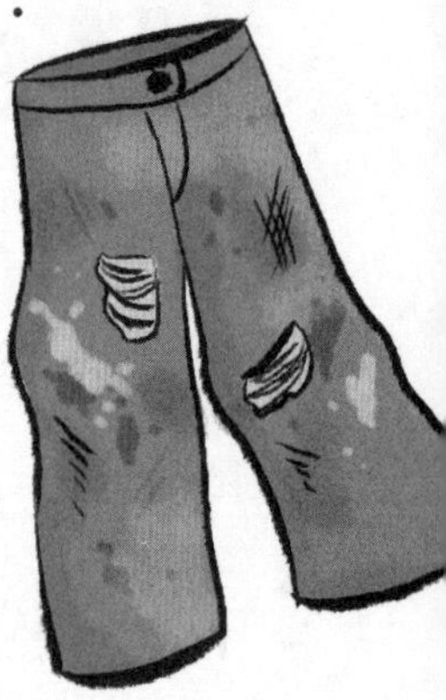

Maddie laughed. "Nope, I just made some updates. Remember my 'painting pants'?"

Emily nodded. She and Maddie had clothing they always wore when they were crafting.

Maddie spun in a circle. "Ta-da!"

Emily couldn't believe it. The jeans that used to have streaks and splotches of paint all over were now bright green. And instead of the streaks and splotches, there were now patches and buttons! Maddie explained that she had bleached the jeans, dyed them green, and then sewn on all the accessories.

"So cool," Emily replied.

Unlike Maddie, Emily was happiest in her overalls. Instead of accessories, they had a million pockets for her tools and tidbits.

Although their outfits were different, they had one thing in common: matching friendship bracelets. The girls had made them together, and they never took the bracelets off their wrists.

Just then the bell rang. Emily and Maddie scrambled to take their seats. Emily sat between Maddie and a boy named Sam Sharma. Sam was pretty quiet, but Emily knew he liked to draw. She knew

because occasionally she'd peek over at his notebook. It was always filled with doodles and drawings. He drew everything from robots to giraffes to spaceships—he even created entire worlds.

Emily was about to tell Sam she loved the forest he was drawing when Ms. Gibbons, their teacher, entered the room.

With her was a girl Emily and Maddie had never seen before. The girl had short dark hair, big brown eyes, and a purple backpack that had numbers and symbols written all over it.

"Class," said Ms. Gibbons, "I'd like you to meet Isabella Diaz. She's a new student here at Birding Creek Elementary, and she'll be joining our class. Let's all do our best to make Isabella feel welcome."

The new girl smiled shyly and

then whispered something to Ms. Gibbons.

"Of course," replied Ms. Gibbons. "Isabella just told me that she goes by Bella, so please, everyone, make *Bella* feel welcome. Bella, why don't you take the seat next to Maddie? Raise your hand, Maddie."

Maddie waved enthusiastically, and Bella went to sit down. "Cool backpack," Emily heard Maddie whisper. "And I love your key chain."

Emily was about to chime in when she heard Bella whisper back, "Thanks. I made it."

"No way," said Maddie. "Can you show me how?"

"Sure!" said Bella.

Emily looked down at her friendship bracelet and twirled it on her wrist. She knew Maddie was just being friendly and doing what Ms. Gibbons had asked. And Bella seemed nice enough.

No one could come between MAD-ILY . . . right?

CHAPTER 2

You sell 8 cookies.
Your friend sells 13.

How many do you s
altogether?

Left Out at Lunch

Later that morning, it was math time. “As you all know, our charity bake sale is in a couple of weeks,” said Ms. Gibbons. “Let’s polish up our math skills so we can be sure to give customers correct change. Maddie, would you be Bella’s partner for math today?”

Emily looked up, surprised. She

considered reminding Ms. Gibbons that she and Maddie always worked together. But before she could raise her hand, she heard Maddie's voice.

"Of course!"

Emily watched as Maddie and Bella pushed their desks together.

It makes Maddie happy to help people, Emily reminded herself. *Plus, Ms. Gibbons probably chose Maddie because she knows I'm good with numbers and can work without a partner.*

Emily tried to be a good sport, but seeing Maddie and Bella whispering and laughing made her heart sink. And her stomach rumble. *Thank goodness it's almost lunchtime,* thought Emily.

In the cafeteria, Emily joined the hot lunch line. Maddie and Bella had both brought lunch. They made a beeline to the tables with their lunch boxes.

"Save me a seat!" Emily called after them.

When Emily finally made it to the table, she was glad to see an empty seat. But when she slid into it, Maddie barely noticed. She was too busy telling Bella about a science experiment disaster.

"No way!" said Bella, laughing.

"It's true!" Maddie insisted. "It just went *fwoosh* and sprayed everything! I was completely soaked."

Emily was about to remind Maddie of another story when she suddenly smelled something . . . amazing.

"Wow," Emily said. "Bella, is that your lunch?"

"Mmm-hmm," said Bella. "It's roasted corn salad and a vegetable quesadilla. My dad is the chef at the

Mexican restaurant El Gallo," she explained.

"You're so lucky!" said Maddie. "My parents can't even make a decent peanut butter sandwich!"

"Neither can mine!" said Bella. "My dad's a great chef, but the one thing he always messes up are PB&Js. It's like they're too easy. So I make them myself."

Maddie laughed. "That reminds me of the time I tried to make chocolate-chip pancakes," she said.

While Maddie elaborated, Emily finished her food silently and stood up.

She waited for a break in the conversation.

And waited.

Finally Emily announced, "I'm going to the art room."

"The art room?" Maddie gave

Emily a funny look. The girls had spent years begging their art teacher, Mrs. Lee, to use the art room after hours. And Mrs. Lee had finally told Emily and Maddie that they could use the room whenever they wanted! But the girls always went *together*.

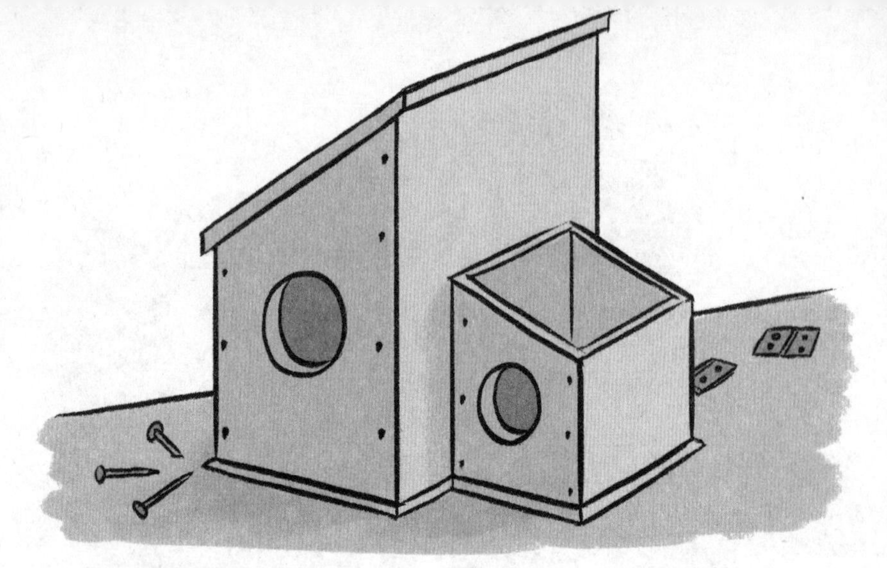

Emily nodded. She was about to tell Maddie about the birdhouse she was building. But just then Maddie turned back to Bella. “Wait. I have to tell you about the time I tried to make tomato soup!” she said.

Emily sighed and cleared her tray. Alone, she headed for the art room.

CHAPTER
3

The *Un*-Friendship Bracelet

The next day Emily brought lunch from home so she could sit down at the exact same time as Maddie and Bella. But once again the other girls chatted nonstop and Emily felt invisible. When Emily finished eating, she went back to the art room.

The following day at lunch, Emily retreated to the art room

even sooner. Mrs. Lee often left the radio on, which made the art room feel extra cozy and homey. Plus Emily was really enjoying seeing her birdhouse project progress.

On Thursday, Emily didn't even sit down in the cafeteria. She just took her lunch to the art room and

got to work as soon as she finished her sandwich.

When everyone returned to the classroom after lunch, Emily noticed something new on Bella's wrist.

"Where'd you get that bracelet?" Emily asked.

"Oh, it's a friendship bracelet! Just like yours!" Bella said excitedly. "Maddie made this one for me. But she taught me how to make them myself too."

Emily's stomach did a flip-flop, but she didn't say anything. Maddie was teaching *Bella* how to make friendship bracelets now?

On Friday morning the class had art. Emily was adding a few details to her birdhouse when she heard someone say, "Whoa! That's awesome."

She turned and was surprised to see Maddie admiring her work.

"Thanks," said Emily. "I've been working on it all week. See, this is where birds can perch, and then this chamber is for bird food."

"So creative," said Maddie. "Want to get together tomorrow? I was thinking we could make friendship bracelets for the charity bake sale."

When Emily looked confused, Maddie laughed. "Not to eat," she said. "Cookies are awesome, but wouldn't it be cool to make something totally unique?"

Emily thought about it. It *was* a great idea. And she especially liked the thought of working on a project, just her and Maddie. But then she remembered something. "Ugh! I have a soccer tournament

this weekend," she told Maddie. "So . . . I can't."

"Can't what?" asked Bella, coming over.

Maddie explained her idea for the bake sale.

"That's such a good idea!" said Bella enthusiastically. "Do you guys need help?"

"Actually, Emily has soccer this weekend," Maddie told

Bella. "But I could definitely use some help! Let's make a plan later!"

That weekend, at the soccer tournament, Emily felt totally off. *I wonder what they're doing right now*, she kept thinking.

"Wake up, Emily!" one of her

teammates yelled as the ball and several players flew past her.

When the final whistle blew, Emily trudged off the field. Usually she'd average two or three goals per game. Today she hadn't scored a single one. She reached for her water bottle—

And gasped! Her wrist was bare. The friendship bracelet Emily always wore—the one that matched Maddie's, that they'd made together, that represented MAD-ILY—was gone.

Emily searched the field, running up and down it. But the bracelet was nowhere to be found.

You can make a new one, she tried to reassure herself. But she couldn't help worrying that maybe the bracelet's disappearance wasn't an accident.

Maybe it was a sign. Maybe her friendship bracelet was actually . . . an *un*-friendship bracelet.

CHAPTER
4

Hidden Treasure!

When the doorbell rang on Saturday afternoon, Bella glanced nervously around the room. Was everything ready? Was everything perfect? Bella was worried that her new home, which didn't even have all the furniture moved in yet, would look bad and boring to her new friend.

But her worries disappeared when she opened the door and saw Maddie holding a tower of crafting supplies. Bella laughed and led her into the dining room. Maddie spread out her supplies on every available surface.

"I love your house!" said Maddie.

"Thanks!" said Bella. "My parents have been making my brother and me unpack boxes for, like, *ever*. So . . . let's see what you brought!"

"Okay," said Maddie, "I've got my bracelet-making materials, but I also brought some other jewelry-making supplies. And I couldn't forget my button collection—I've made some amazing bracelets out of buttons. Bottlecaps, too, see?"

Bella admired all of Maddie's creations, and the two girls quickly got to work. The afternoon flew by as they assembled bracelet after bracelet in all colors of the rainbow.

“Are you hungry?” Bella asked Maddie.

Maddie nodded. “Is your dad going to whip us up something awesome?”

“He’s at work,” said Bella. “But if we make popcorn, we can put his homemade spice mix on it.”

“Perfect!” said Maddie.

When the two girls had assembled a big bowl of popcorn and two ice-cold glasses of lemonade, they suddenly noticed there was no room to enjoy their snack. The table was completely covered with bracelets and crafting supplies.

"We can sit in the backyard," suggested Bella, leading the way.

As they stepped outside, Maddie noticed a small, rickety structure behind Bella's house. "What's that?" she asked.

Bella shrugged. "I guess it's a shed? We just moved in, so I haven't checked it out yet."

S
W

"Really?" said Maddie. "But it could be filled with hidden treasure! Gold or diamonds . . ."

"Or bugs and snakes," suggested Bella.

Maddie shuddered at the thought.

"But," said Bella, "we'll never know unless we look."

The two girls examined the door to the shed. There was a latch, but no lock, so they were able to get the door open.

Bella fumbled around and then flicked on the light switch. The two girls gasped at what they saw.

It wasn't snakes or bugs. It was . . . *stuff*. Ropes, tools, wood, paints, glass jars of buttons, nuts, bolts and other fasteners, bicycle wheels, chains, planters, and so much more!

"Whoa!" said Bella.

"I know!" said Maddie. "I thought there might be treasure, but I had no idea it would be *this* amazing! Look at all this cool stuff! And so much of it. Where do we even start?"

"Probably by cleaning it out," said Bella, running a finger through the dust on a shelf. "That is, if my parents let us."

"Are you going to ask them?" asked Maddie. When Bella nodded, Maddie grinned. "And you know who's going to be just as excited as we are?"

"Who?" asked Bella.

"Emily! I can't wait to tell her the news!"

CHAPTER
5

The Inside Joke

On Monday, Emily got to school early. She wondered if she should have worn a long-sleeved shirt so Maddie wouldn't notice that her bracelet was missing. Emily hadn't seen or talked to Maddie since Friday. Her mom mentioned that Maddie had called while Emily was at the tournament, but Emily was so tired on

Sunday night that she went to bed right after finishing her homework.

Emily looked up as kids filed into the classroom. Bella waved to Emily, and Maddie flashed her a big grin.

"How'd the bracelet making go?" asked Emily when the girls sat down.

"Awesome," said Maddie. "Wait until we show you!"

The hands on the clock seemed to be moving very slowly that morning. Finally the recess bell rang and the girls went outside to the playground. Maddie pulled a big box out of her bag and lifted the lid. It was stuffed to the brim with bracelets.

"Wow!" said Emily. "You guys made so many!"

"And we're not even done yet," said Maddie. "We're just getting started, really."

Emily was about to offer to help when Bella added, "We *would* have made more if it hadn't been for—"

"Marco!" Maddie groaned.

"Who's Marco?" asked Emily.

"He's my big brother," explained Bella. "He said we were making them too small. . . ."

"Because he thought they were dog collars, not bracelets."

"Yeah, he was all—"

"No, no, he was like—"

Bella and Maddie started to talk over each other, laughing the whole time. Emily touched her wrist where her friendship bracelet would have been. It didn't matter what shirt she was wearing. Maddie certainly wasn't going to notice that her bracelet was missing.

CHAPTER
6

Sam's Big Ideas

When Emily slid back into her seat before recess ended, she was surprised to find Sam already in his seat, drawing. Out of habit, she glanced over to see what he was creating.

She gasped. Sam had created a huge, incredibly detailed city of birdhouses. In the sky he had

drawn all sorts of birds. And each bird had a different kind of home!

Emily tapped Sam on the shoulder.

Startled, Sam covered his note-book.

"Sorry!" said Emily. "I just wanted to tell you that I like your picture. Plus, I think it's *extra* cool because I'm making a birdhouse in the art room. That's where it is now."

"Really?" said Sam.

Emily nodded. "I designed and built it myself. Though it would be cooler if it looked like that!" she said, pointing at Sam's drawing.

"Maybe I could help you with it," suggested Sam.

“That would be great!” said Emily.

At lunchtime Emily waited for Sam, and then they headed for the art room together. Sam’s eyes grew wide when he saw Emily’s birdhouse.

“That’s awesome!” he said. “It would be fun to paint the base yellow. And you could make both sides of the roof go all the way down, then curve up, sort of like wings?”

“Great idea,” said Emily.

“Thanks! But it’s already pretty cool,” Sam told her. “I wish I could build things like this. I guess I’m better at drawing and painting.”

“I could help you with that,” Emily replied. She got out some tools, and Sam gathered paints. Together, they worked on adding pieces to the roof. They *did* sort of look like bird wings!

“Hey, can I ask you something?” Sam said as he carefully painted the base of the birdhouse.

“Sure,” said Emily.

“Where’s Maddie?” Sam asked.

"You guys are always together."

"Yeah . . . ," Emily said, trailing off. Then she told Sam how Maddie seemed to only want to hang out with Bella now. And how Maddie had made a friendship bracelet for Bella. "And meanwhile," Emily continued, "*my* friendship bracelet fell off last weekend and it's lost forever. So I guess it's official: Bella and Maddie are friends, and I'm not."

"Why don't you ask Maddie to help you make another one?" asked Sam.

"I don't know," admitted Emily.

"You should," encouraged Sam. "And maybe tell her you feel left out. Sometimes people have no idea how you feel unless you tell them." Sam was now painting designs on top of the yellow.

Emily stood back and admired their work. Sam's design ideas were really terrific. His friendship ideas were pretty good too. She decided to take his advice and talk to Maddie in the morning.

CHAPTER
7

Time to Tell the Truth

The next day Emily kept glancing at Maddie's desk, waiting for her to appear. *She's probably just running late,* Emily thought. But by the time the bell for recess rang, Maddie still hadn't arrived at school.

On the playground Emily saw Bella sitting by herself with a little notebook.

“Do you know where Maddie is?” Emily asked Bella.

“No,” said Bella. “I was going to ask you. Maybe when we go back in we can see if Ms. Gibbons knows.”

“Okay,” said Emily. She was about to walk away when she saw that Bella had been writing something in her notebook. "What are you writing?" she asked.

Bella looked embarrassed. "Oh, just some calculations."

"Calculations?" said Emily excitedly. "Like math?"

"Part math and part science," explained Bella. "Have you ever made a potato clock?"

"Um, no," said Emily. "Tell me more!"

The two girls huddled over Bella's notebook. They were so

focused on their conversation that they both jumped at the sound of Emily's name.

It was Sam. "What planet were you on, Emily? I must have called your name ten times," he said with a laugh.

"Sorry!" said Emily. "Bella was just showing me the coolest thing. Bella, this is Sam. He's an amazing artist and helped me turn my birdhouse into a bird *palace*. And, Sam, this is Bella. She's a coding and circuitry wizard. Look at this!"

Emily pointed at Bella's notebook,

but as she did, Bella noticed Emily's wrist.

"Emily, where's your friendship bracelet? The one you always wear?"

Just then the bell rang.

"I . . . uh . . . ," Emily stammered,

getting up. “I lost it at soccer last weekend. I looked all over, but it was gone.”

“Want me to make you a new one?” offered Bella.

“That’s okay,” said Emily. She knew Bella was just trying to be nice, but what she really wanted was her special MAD-ILY bracelet. The one she and Maddie had made together.

After school Emily's mom picked her up. She agreed to drive by Maddie's house so Emily could check on her.

When Emily rang the Wilsons' doorbell, the door swung open. There stood Maddie in her pajamas.

"Hi!" said Maddie, hugging Emily. "Don't worry. I'm not contagious."

"Where were you today?" Emily asked, relieved to see that her friend was okay.

"I woke up feeling yucky," Maddie explained. "But by lunchtime I was okay. My parents kept me home just

to be on the safe side. And I'm *sooo* glad to see you!"

"Me too," said Emily, and she meant it. Maddie's mom invited Emily's mom in for tea while the two girls caught up.

"I've been feeling a little yucky lately too," Emily admitted. "Not sick, though. Just . . . left out."

"You have?" Maddie asked in surprise. "Why?"

Emily took a deep breath and explained everything.

"Wow," said Maddie. "Emily, I'm so sorry! I didn't mean to make you feel left out at all."

"I know," said Emily. "You would never do that on purpose."

At that moment the phone rang. It was Bella. Emily felt the flip-flop feeling return to her stomach as Maddie chatted happily. But she reminded herself that she'd had a lot of fun with Bella at recess.

Maddie hung up the phone. "Guess what?" she said excitedly. Then she told Emily all about the shed full of treasures. "And Bella just invited both of us to start cleaning it out!"

"Cool!" Emily exclaimed. Then she had an idea. "Can we make one stop on the way?"

When Maddie nodded, Emily borrowed a phone and their classroom directory.

"Hello, Sam?" she said. "Are you busy? There is something my friends and I want to show you."

CHAPTER
8

Crafty Cleanup!

“So, what’s in this thing?” said Sam, peering inside the shed.

“You’ll see!” said Bella, flipping on the light.

“Ohh. I love creepy, crawly—Whoa!” cried Sam. “This is even better than I could have imagined!”

“It’s amazing,” agreed Emily. Everywhere she looked there were

tools and pieces of scrap wood, chicken wire, metal, and other building supplies.

"Let's get started!" said Bella. "This shed is not going to clean itself, as my mom would say."

So the kids decided to sort every-

thing into piles. Building supplies in one, tools in another, paints in another, knickknacks in another, and so on.

"Where should I put this sketchbook?" asked Maddie, holding it up.

"Oh, that's mine," said Sam.

“Can I see?” Bella asked. Sam shrugged and opened it to a random page. A jungle burst forth, with tropical plants, insects, and monkeys.

“That is so cool,” said Bella as Emily and Maddie joined them.

Sam flipped through the sketchbook, feeling more confident now and describing his inspiration for the art inside.

Maddie pointed out a bright butterfly. "I sewed a butterfly costume for my little sister for Halloween last year," she said.

Bella pointed to some gears Sam had drawn. "I think we have some gears like this in the knickknacks pile. I bet I can figure out something to make with them!"

Emily smiled. This day sure was turning out better than it started.

It took the kids the rest of the week to clean out the shed. On Saturday afternoon a ray of sunlight came pouring through the shed's windows, filling the space with a happy glow.

"Wow, look at it now!" said Bella.

The other three kids nodded in agreement. The space had been transformed. It seemed a lot bigger, empty. And all their treasures were sitting in bins and bags, just waiting to be used.

"Hey, Bella?" asked Emily. "What's the shed going to be used for now?"

Bella shrugged her shoulders. "Beats me. Why?"

Emily looked around thoughtfully. "Well, it looks to me like the perfect crafting studio. That is, if you know any kids who like to draw and build and sew and make stuff. . . ."

"We do!" Maddie, Bella, and Sam all shouted at once.

By the time everyone went home for dinner, they had a plan. Over the weekend Bella would ask her family for permission. If the answer was yes, they would all meet at recess on Monday to discuss and draw up plans for their awesome new studio.

CHAPTER
9

Sew, Paint, Build, Repeat

At school on Monday, Maddie, Emily, and Sam ran to greet Bella.

"So, what did your parents say?" asked Maddie excitedly.

Bella frowned. "They didn't like the idea," she said.

"Oh no!" said Emily.

Slowly, the corners of Bella's mouth turned up. "They didn't like

it," she repeated. "They *loved* it!"

Maddie, Emily, and Sam stared at Bella for a moment. Then they realized what she had just said and they started cheering.

The kids spent recess brainstorming ideas for the studio: everything from a chalkboard wall to an indoor swing to a foldout desk with room for sewing and working on a computer.

After school they gathered at Bella's house.

"Okay, what should we do first?" asked Maddie.

"Worktable?" suggested Bella.

"I'm on it!" said Emily. She showed the others how to measure twice, sand surfaces, secure

corners, and determine if the top was level. "Ta-da!" she said finally. "Ready for a coat of paint."

"I think I can handle that," said Sam with a smile. "Speaking of painting, what if we did a mural on one wall?" He showed them a sketch.

Maddie clapped her hands with excitement. “I know what else we could make.” She pulled out a bolt of fabric. “Floor cushions! To make it cozy, especially when we need a break.”

"And how about a potato clock so we can keep track of time?" said Bella. She ran back into the house, came out with two potatoes, and demonstrated how to connect them with wire to an old digital clock that didn't have batteries.

"Aren't you worried we'll end up with *baked* potatoes?" asked Emily with a wink.

Everyone laughed.

Suddenly Emily remembered something. She still had not replaced her missing friendship bracelet. *I'll tell Maddie soon*, she thought.

Every afternoon for the rest of the week, the kids met up at Bella's house to work on transforming the shed into a crafting studio. It was a lot of work: building, drawing, painting, and creating. Sam sketched his mural on the wall with chalk, and all four of them painted. Maddie

pinned together curtains and taught the others to sew seams and attach rickrack, pom-poms, and fringe. Emily continued to build furniture with Bella's assistance, and Bella set up her computer. "After all," she

pointed out, "coding is crafting too."

"It is?" asked Sam.

"Sure," said Bella. "It's all about being creative and making stuff. Plus, why else would they call it Mine*craft*?"

CHAPTER 10

Friends New and Old!

By Sunday afternoon Maddie's new painting pants were as speckled and splattered as her old pair had been. Bella came running out of the house with a bandage for Emily's newest scratch.

"Ouch," she said sympathetically.

"Yeah," said Emily. "It was worth it, though."

"I'll say!" said Sam. "This place is amazing!"

The kids admired their work. They had created a Sewing Station and a Coding Corner. The sewing machine was bolted to the tabletop, but you could flip the table up to create more workspace. Bella had made sure the computer had high-speed Internet by repositioning her family's router. There was Sam's Painting Pavilion, which was lined with all different color paints and about a million brushes of different

sizes. Emily's Carpentry Cabinet had tons of tools and materials. The shed already had a working sink, but the kids had added shelving for all their supplies. Plus, they'd painted a chalkboard wall and added that swing!

"Well," said Maddie, "I guess all there is left to do is . . . make stuff! What should we create first?"

Suddenly Bella gasped. “The charity bake sale!” she remembered. “It’s in a couple of days!”

“Oh no! The friendship bracelets!” said Emily. “We got so busy setting up the studio, we forgot to make more!”

Sam looked at the girls, utterly confused.

"To sell, not to eat," Emily explained. "Maddie and Bella made a bunch, but we need more if we're going to have enough for the bake sale."

"Well, can you teach me?" asked Sam. "With four of us, it should go pretty fast."

"Great idea!" said Bella. "Here, watch. This is how Maddie showed me." She selected four strands of embroidery thread, tied a knot, and

taped it to the big worktable.

"Slow down!" said Sam with a laugh. But he caught on quickly. He copied Bella's movements. Emily and Maddie joined them at the table and started making bracelets too. Before long they were tying off the bracelets' ends.

Suddenly Emily felt a tap on her shoulder. She turned and saw that Maddie was holding out something for her.

It was the most beautiful bracelet she had ever seen. Emily turned it over in her hand, admiring it.

"The other day I noticed that you weren't wearing your bracelet," Maddie explained. "I sort of figured you'd lost it but maybe didn't want to tell me?"

Emily nodded in disbelief.

"Well, I made you a new one. See? The four colors represent each

of us. And we can make one for Sam, too!" said Maddie.

Emily beamed as Maddie tied the brand-new bracelet on her wrist.

The four kids spent the rest of the afternoon making bracelets, laughing, and talking about future projects.

As Emily tied knot after knot, she smiled to herself. She was so glad she had talked to Maddie about her feelings. The two girls were still as close as ever. And to top it all off, Emily had made two *new* friends! So much for that *un*-friendship bracelet!

How to Make . . .
A Friendship Bracelet

What you need:

Embroidery thread (four colors!)
Scissors
Tape

Cut four strands of embroidery thread (one of each color) about twelve inches long.

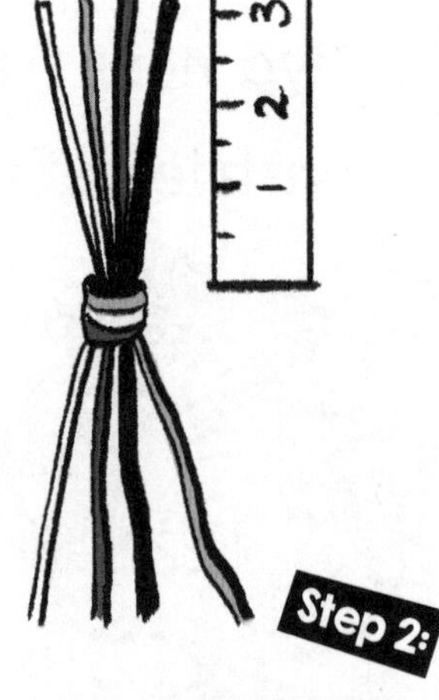

Step 2:

Holding the strands by one end, tie them all together with a knot, leaving about three inches above the knot.

Tape the loose three inches to a table or other surface where you can work.

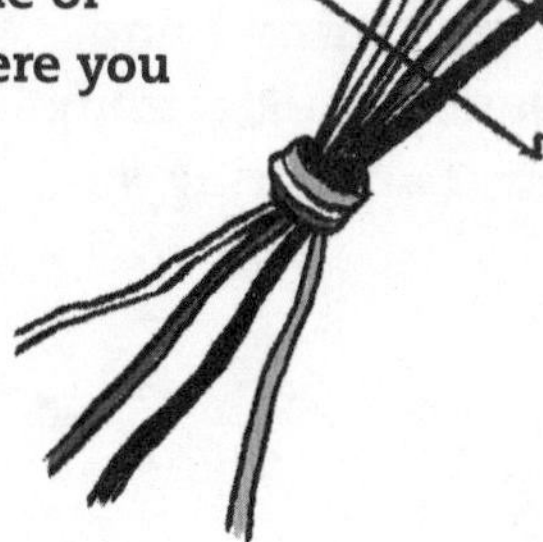

Step 4:

Start with string 1 and loop it over, then under string 2. Make sure you hold string 2 straight. Pull the knot you made with string 1 tight.

Do Step 4 again so you have a double knot.

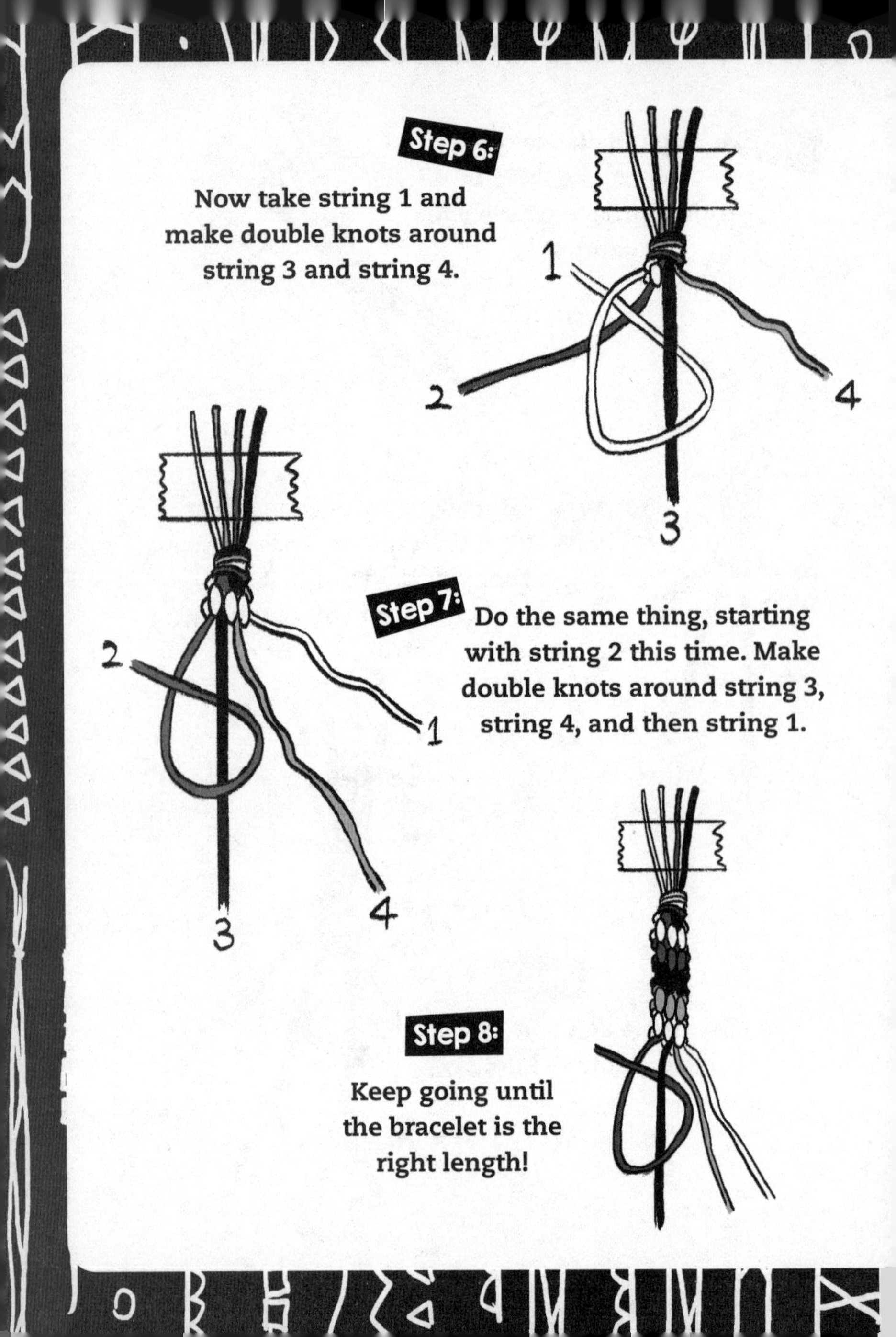
Step 6:
Now take string 1 and make double knots around string 3 and string 4.
1
2
3
4
2
1
3
4
Step 7:
Do the same thing, starting with string 2 this time. Make double knots around string 3, string 4, and then string 1.
Step 8:
Keep going until the bracelet is the right length!

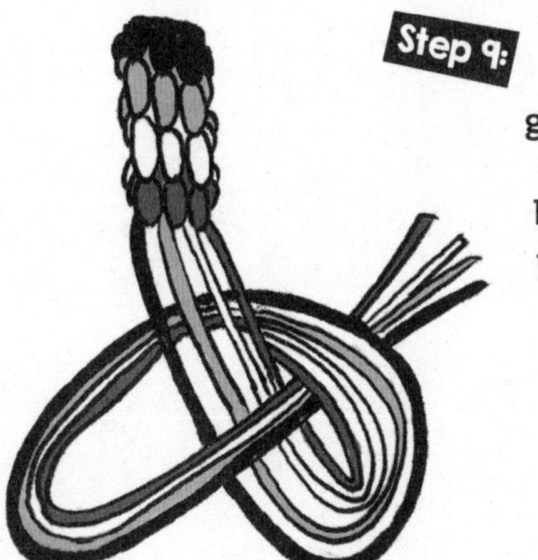

Step 9:

When you're done, gather the ends together and tie a knot so the bracelet is secure. Then trim the ends but leave one inch.

Step 10:

Tie the two ends together to make a bracelet!

Making the Band

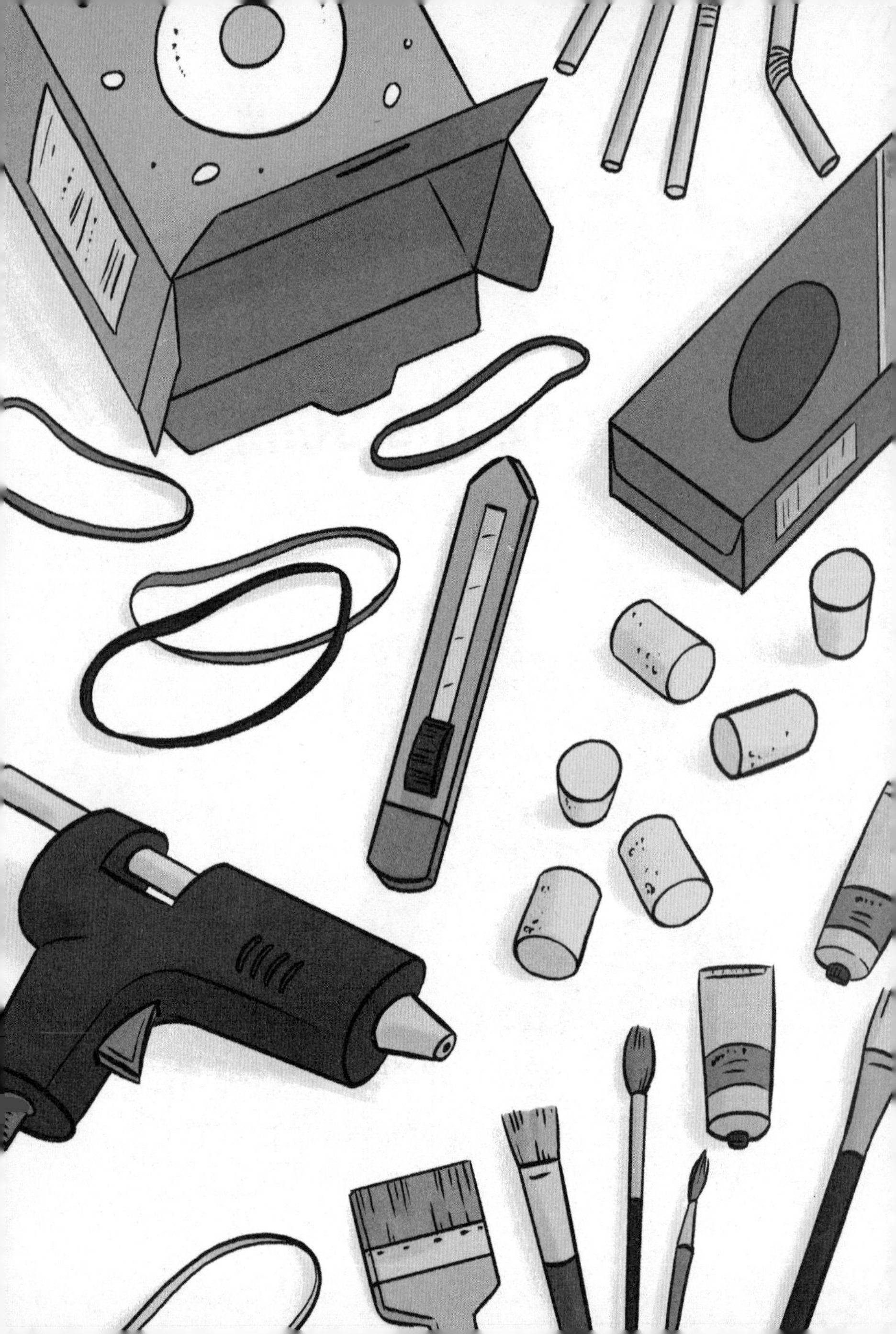

CONTENTS

CHAPTER
1

It's a . . . Brushbot!

"Should we just . . . start?" Bella Diaz asked, glancing at her watch.

"Let's wait a few more minutes," Emily Adams suggested.

"Yeah," agreed Maddie Wilson.

The three friends were at their craft clubhouse—formerly known as the old shed in Bella's backyard. Usually, it was *four* friends, but Sam Sharma was nowhere in sight.

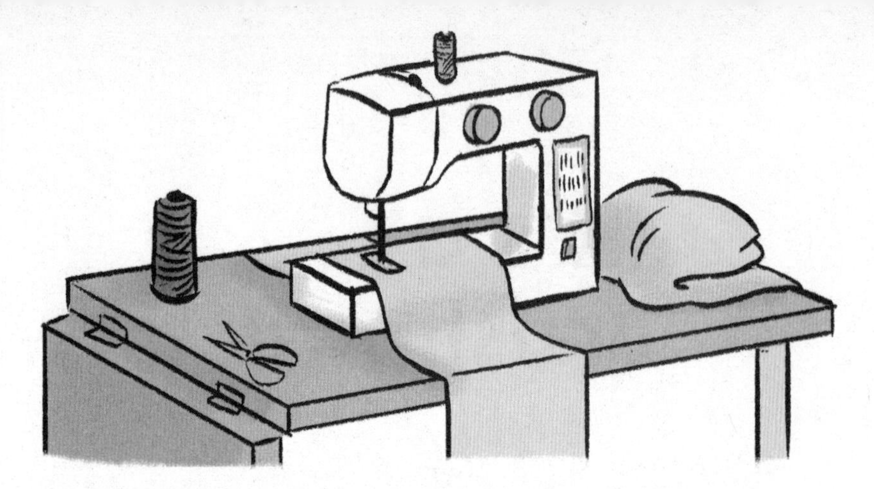

The craft clubhouse was filled with all sorts of materials the kids used for their crafty projects. They had a Sewing Station, where Maddie could often be found. There was a Coding Corner, with a computer that Bella had installed. Emily's Carpentry Cabinet contained

tons of tools, gadgets, and materials like nuts and bolts. And Sam's Painting Pavilion housed different color paints and about a million brushes of different sizes.

But where *was* Sam?

"Sorry I am late!" someone shouted as the shed door flew open. *There* was Sam, breathless. "I had to clean my hamster's cage. It takes forever!" he explained.

Maddie nodded sympathetically. "I know what that's like," she said.

"I mean, having to do chores. It's my job to set the dinner table *every* night!"

"You're both lucky," said Bella. "Since my dad is a chef, he uses every pot and pan when he cooks. And guess who has to clean up? *But* the other night, doing the dishes actually gave me an amazing idea for a new crafting project. Behold!"

Bella handed an object to each of her friends.

"Scrub brushes?" asked Sam, confused.

"Right now, yes," said Bella. "But we're going to transform them into: Brushbots!"

Bella opened her notebook to a diagram. "A Brushbot is a battery-powered scrub brush that can move on its own," she explained.

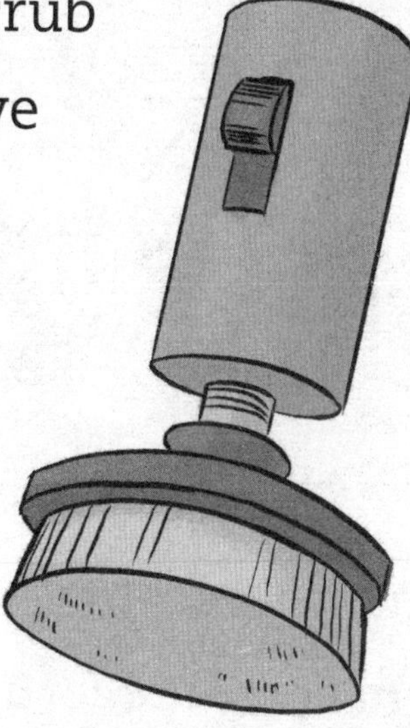

"And sort of looks like a robot! That's genius!" exclaimed Sam.

The first step was for each of them to attach a battery pack to a scrub brush. The kids continued working, carefully following Bella's instructions.

“Before we decorate them, let’s try them out!” Bella suggested. “On the count of three. One, two . . .”

“THREE!” everyone yelled, flipping the switches.

Nothing happened.

“What did we do wrong?” Maddie asked.

"Maybe these batteries are duds?" suggested Emily.

Bella looked concerned. "But they're brand-new," she said.

"Are they the *right* kind of batteries?" asked Sam.

Bella pulled out a battery and examined it. Then she started to

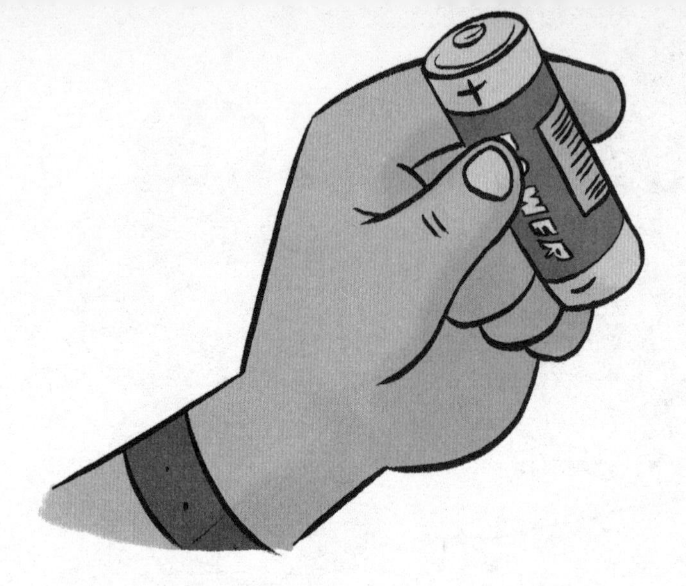

laugh. “I think I know what went wrong. You see how each battery has a plus sign at one end and a minus at the other?”

The other three nodded.

“Well, to make the connection, positive and negative need to be in the right positions. Once we do that . . .”

The friends rotated the batteries and flipped the switches. The Brushbots started working immediately!

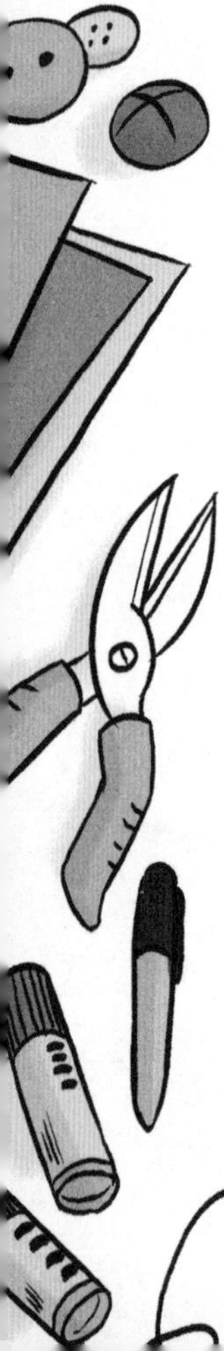

Next they got to work on decorations. The hours flew by as they glued, sewed, and painted. When they were done, they set the Brushbots on a shelf to dry. Sam's looked like a metal insect, with bug eyes and antennae cut from an old hanger. Maddie's was wear-ing a beret and a coordinated outfit. Emily's had nuts and bolts glued on in cool patterns. And Bella's looked like a real robot, with electric wires wrapping around in all different directions.

"Bring on the dirty dishes!" said Bella.

Maddie laughed. "I think I like mine too much to use it for chores!" she admitted.

Emily and Sam nodded in agreement.

"You guys!" said Bella, though she knew her friends were right. Her Brushbot *had* turned out really cool too.

Looked like she'd have to keep doing the dinner dishes the old-fashioned way . . . for now.

CHAPTER
2

What's *Your* Talent?

At school the next day, the kids gathered for the Monday-morning assembly. Onstage, their principal, Ms. Park, began announcements.

"I have some exciting news!" she said. "Mason Creek Elementary will be hosting a school-wide talent show. Students can participate on their own or in groups."

Bella, Emily, Maddie, and Sam exchanged knowing looks. Sure, they would need to figure out what to do, but even without discussing it they knew they would work on their act together.

Principal Park continued, saying, "You can perform a song or a dance, read a story or a poem, juggle, or even help out backstage. This is an exciting event that will showcase the talents of our entire school community!"

At recess, the four friends gathered on the playground.

"What should we do for the talent show?" asked Maddie.

"*Not* singing, please," said Bella. "I don't even sound good when I sing in the shower," she added with a sheepish smile.

"Not dancing, either," said Emily. "My fancy footwork is strictly for the soccer field."

"I'm going to twirl my baton," their classmate Joelle said, marching by and flipping her baton into the air to demonstrate.

"I'm going to do magic," proclaimed Lyle, another classmate. He pulled out a deck of cards and fanned them in front of the friends.

"And I'll be his magician's assistant!" said Lyle's best friend, Cory.

Alana and Kai, two other classmates, came running up. “Maddie!” said Alana. “We’re going to write a play for the talent show. Would you do the costumes?”

Maddie was really flattered. "I'm sorry!" she said. "But I already have a group."

"That's okay! What are you guys doing?" asked Kai.

The four friends looked at each other.

"Well . . . we're not sure yet," Sam finally answered.

Kai frowned, then brightened up. "I'm sure it will be something great!" she said enthusiastically.

The school bell rang just then, and Kai and Alana hurried off.

"So . . . meet at the craft clubhouse after school?" Bella asked.

The other three kids couldn't have said "Yes!" faster.

CHAPTER
3

Out of Ideas

That afternoon at Bella's house, the four friends grabbed their go-to snack—lemonade and a big bowl of popcorn with Bella's dad's special spice blend on it—and trooped out to the craft clubhouse.

"Brainstorming time!" Maddie said. "And just remember, like Ms. Gibbons always says . . ."

"'When you brainstorm, there are no bad ideas,'" everyone said together, repeating one of their teacher's favorite sayings.

"I'll make a list," offered Sam.

"No singing," Bella reminded him.

“And no dancing,” added Emily.

“So far this is a list of things we’re *not* doing,” Sam pointed out.

Bella sighed. “Well, we can’t exactly code a computer game onstage,” she said.

Emily nodded in agreement. “Or build a tree house,” she added.

"Guys, I hear you," said Maddie patiently. "But let's keep thinking. I'm sure something great will come to us. Like, we could do a fashion show."

"Or paint something together," suggested Sam. "I'm not sure *how*, but I'm going to write it down anyway." He added his idea and Maddie's to the list.

"Hmm . . . we could build a robot and show how it works onstage?" Bella said.

"Or something out of wood might be a little easier?" Emily added.

"This is a good start," said Sam, after adding both ideas. "My dad will be here soon to take me to my art class, so here's our list so far. Add more ideas if you think of any, okay?"

He pinned the list to the club-house wall and then left to meet his dad.

The girls crowded around to take a look.

Finally, Emily spoke. She said what everyone was thinking: "There aren't any *bad* ideas here. But I'm not sure there are any *great* ideas yet, either."

CHAPTER
4

Inspiration Strikes!

When Sam got home after art class, dinner was almost ready. His little sister, Yasmin, was at the table drawing.

"Hi, Mom! Hi, Yazzy!" called Sam. He hung up his backpack and kicked off his sneakers.

Sam quickly set the table and gave Yasmin a piece of naan to

nibble so she wouldn't complain when he swapped her paper and crayons for a place mat and dishes.

"Such a busy day at work today!" said Sam's mom, who was a high-school art teacher. She carried a steaming bowl of chana masala to the table. Sam's mouth watered. Usually he didn't like chickpeas. But somehow his mom made them delicious!

"You should have been an architect instead of a teacher," teased his dad. "Much less stressful."

"Oh, really? What about that time you cut your finger building that model of the museum?"

Sam's parents laughed.

"When you guys were in school together," said Sam, "did you ever have to do a talent show?"

"Sure," said his dad. "At *our*

school talent show, I got everyone on their feet with my rock and roll."

"You did?" Sam was impressed.

"Kind of," admitted Sam's dad. "Mostly because they got up to use the bathroom when I played. I was pretty bad. Your mom's the real musician."

"*You* played rock music?" Sam asked his mom.

She smiled. "Classical guitar and jazz."

"I really want to find something I can do with my friends," Sam said. "We tried to figure it out today, but we just don't have any good ideas."

“Give it time,” said Sam’s mother gently.

“Inspiration can strike when you least expect it,” added his dad.

Sam waited for inspiration to strike all through dinner. He waited for it as he helped clear the table.

He waited for it through his science homework, then math.

Stumped by a division problem, Sam began tapping his pencil. *Come on, inspiration. Where are you?* he thought.

"You about ready to call it a night, Sam?"

Sam looked up and saw his dad standing in the doorway. "Oh. Uh, sure. Just a few more math problems."

"Okay," said his dad. "Nice beat."

"Beat?" Sam looked down and realized that he was still tapping his pencil against the desk.

"Sounds good. You're already a better drummer than I was a guitar player," his dad said.

Sam grinned. Then, all of a sudden, an idea hit him. If he could make a drum out of a pencil and a desk, maybe he and his friends could create other instruments too! Then they could perform a song while showcasing their crafting talents. And they wouldn't have to sing or dance!

Sam tried to turn his attention back to math, but he kept tapping his pencil excitedly. He couldn't wait to tell his friends!

CHAPTER
5

Cereal Boxes and Jingle Bells

At school the next day, Sam shared his idea.

"I love it!" said Emily.

"Ooh, and we'll need something cool to wear as a band," said Maddie. "I'm on it!"

"Awesome!" said Bella. "What instruments should we make?"

Just then their teacher walked in.

“Come along, everyone,” said Ms. Gibbons. “We have music first today.”

“Perfect!” whispered Bella as the kids lined up. “Now we can look at everything in the music room

and figure out what instruments to make."

The suggestion sounded simple enough. But there were so many different instruments in the music room: triangles, drums, guitars, shakers, tambourines, and more! The four friends all took note of the instruments and how they might re-create them. They didn't have a chance to talk about their ideas for the rest of the day, so they were all excited to meet up at Bella's house later.

"We'll definitely need a guitar," said Bella, putting some home-made cookies on a plate for them to take out to the clubhouse. "I took lessons, so I know how to play. I just have to figure out how to make one."

Sam picked up a wooden spoon from the counter and pretended to play it like a guitar.

"Hey, wait a second!" Emily took the spoon and positioned it by a box of cereal that was nearby. The spoon formed the long neck of the guitar and the box formed its body.

"Awesome!" said Bella. Then she went over to the kitchen recycling bin. "What if instead of the spoon we used this?" She pulled out a long box that had once held spaghetti.

"Oh, and look!" Maddie reached into the recycling bin and pulled out two oatmeal containers. "What could we use these for?"

"Drums!" said Sam instantly.

They carried their cookies and found materials out to the craft clubhouse and got to work. Maddie was still excited about the idea of band outfits, so she dug through the boxes of sewing supplies in search of just the right things.

"What about these?" she asked, pulling out a bag of shiny silver balls.

"Jingle bells?" asked Emily. "Won't we look a little silly, like jesters or elves, if we wear those?"

Maddie laughed. "Not for our outfits," she said. "For an instrument!"

"Ohhhh!" Emily took the bag and shook it. "Right! These remind me of the bell shakers in the music room!"

Emily grabbed two long wooden dowels. "I can drill holes and attach the bells!" she said excitedly.

She took the supplies over to the woodworking bench and put on her safety goggles.

"I guess that just leaves me," said Maddie.

Bella looked up from her work. "There are lots of things you can make, Maddie. You're so talented!"

"I'm sure something will come to you," added Sam. "Inspiration can strike when you least expect it!"

"You guys are probably right," said Maddie. "I'll just keep working on our outfits until I think of something. It would be *terrible* if we didn't look as great as we sounded!"

CHAPTER
6

A Leaky Disaster

By Friday the friends had created an amazing assortment of instruments. Bella had built a guitar out of a cereal box and two pasta boxes. It had rubber-band strings and cork knobs. It also had paperclip frets, so it actually could be played! Sam had a complete oatmeal-canister drum set, plus cymbals made out of paper

plates. In typical Sam fashion, he had painted the drum set with all sorts of patterns and designs in every color imaginable. Emily had made several percussion pieces, including her bell shakers and shakers made out of paper cups filled with dried beans.

"We're going to rock!" said Sam, and the others cheered in agreement.

The only band member who was still instrumentless was Maddie. She kept busy sewing while waiting for inspiration to strike.

On Saturday morning Bella woke up early. She looked outside and noticed that the grass was wet. Really wet. The sun was shining, but it looked like it had probably rained all night.

I'll go see if the glue on my guitar is dry, she thought.

She slipped on her rain boots and sloshed out to the clubhouse. She flung open the door and—

"Oh no!" she cried.

The clubhouse was . . . a disaster. It seemed that the roof had leaked overnight during the rainstorm.

Almost everything in the shed was completely drenched! And that included all their instruments. Bella's guitar was a soggy mess, as were Sam's drums. Emily's noise-makers had fared a little bit better, but not by much. Luckily, Bella's beloved computer seemed fine.

A little while later the other three kids arrived at the clubhouse.

They all gasped when they saw the damage.

"What are we going to do?" asked Bella.

"Well, I say we start by cleaning up," said Emily.

The others agreed. They got to work inspecting the contents of the clubhouse. They threw out what was

damaged and set other things out to dry in the sun. Emily grabbed a ladder and a flashlight and climbed up to examine the roof.

"Be careful!" said Bella. "It's probably slippery up there."

"I don't have to actually go on the roof," Emily reassured her. "I just need to stand on the ladder so I can reach the spot that needs patching."

"I'll help you," offered Maddie. She held the ladder steady, handed up tools, and accepted items that Emily handed down. Emily passed

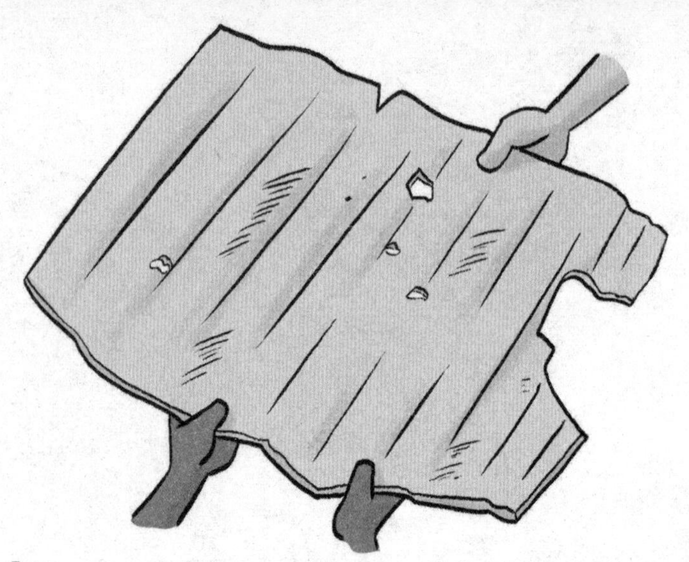

down a big square of corrugated metal that was filled with holes. Clearly *that* was the cause of the leak.

Throughout the morning, the team worked hard on cleaning and repairs. At lunchtime Bella's father brought out a tray of sandwiches, plus tortilla chips and delicious homemade salsa. He also brought something else.

"A can of coffee?" Bella looked confused.

"It's empty," her father said. "I thought it might make a good metal drum? You know, a waterproof one."

"Awesome!" said Sam. "Do you have any other waterproof cans?"

Bella's dad smiled. "Of course! I'm a chef, remember? I have tomato cans, jalapeño pepper cans, and olive oil drums, plus huge plastic containers from the restaurant supply store."

Sam followed Mr. Diaz to the kitchen. When he returned, his arms were full. "These are going

to be even *better* drums than the ones I made before!" he exclaimed.

Seeing Sam with the metal cans, Maddie suddenly had an idea.

"Mr. Diaz?" she asked. "Can I have the piece of metal that came off the roof?"

"What for?" asked Bella.

"Oh, you'll see," said Maddie mysteriously.

CHAPTER
7

Starting All Over

The next week was a busy one as the four friends struggled to repair and replace their damaged instruments. Bella was pleased to find a jumbo-size cereal box in the recycling bin, which made a better guitar body. She found more pasta boxes too. However, she ran into a new problem.

Boing! Boing!

"Ow!" said Sam. A rubber band had popped off Bella's guitar and flown across the room, striking him on the elbow.

"Sorry!" said Bella. *Twang!* Another rubber band broke off her guitar. "I don't know if I can make this work. These rubber bands keep popping off or breaking."

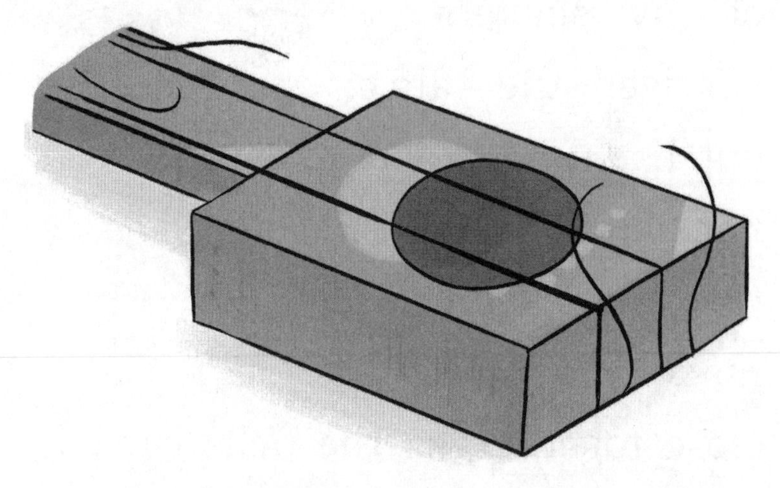

"Have you tried using bigger ones?" asked Sam. "I can bring some in tomorrow. My dad has a whole bunch for rolling up his architectural drawings."

"That would be great!"

"Meanwhile," said Emily, "some of my shakers survived the rain, but listen." She shook her bell shakers while the others listened. "I made the holes too close together, so the bells can't jingle. Guess I'm going to have to start over after all."

"I'm actually glad I had to make new drums," said Sam. "Check this out." He hit his drums in turn.

"They each have a different sound," observed Emily.

"I know," said Sam. "Before, they sounded the same because they were the same material. But these are different sizes and different materials. So now the beats make all sorts of sounds!"

"Maddie, when are you going to show us what *your* instrument is?" asked Bella.

Maddie was hunched over something, her back to her friends. They could see that she was tying a bow around the back of her neck.

"Now!" she said as she turned around.

Maddie was *wearing* the piece of corrugated metal that had come off the roof as if it were a long bib. It hung from a ribbon around her neck. She was holding a metal soup spoon and a wire whisk, which she

proceeded to scrape up and down the zigzag surface of the metal, producing a really cool scratchy sound.

"Wow," said Sam. "What is it?"

"It's called a zydeco washboard," announced Maddie. "My uncle Alvin lives in New Orleans. He plays one

in a band. Emily helped me trim the sides and bend the top edge so it sits right on my shoulders."

"I can't believe it, but our instruments are even better than before!" said Bella. "I guess we have the rain to thank."

"Rain, hard work, patience, and the best friends ever," said Maddie, whisking her washboard with a flourish.

"I think it's about time we start practicing!" suggested Emily.

After all, the talent show was in three days!

CHAPTER
8

Practice, Practice, Practice!

The next day the band members gathered at the Craft Clubhouse, ready to practice.

"Okay, why don't we start with a simple song?" said Bella.

"How about 'Twinkle, Twinkle, Little Star'?" suggested Emily.

"Sure!" said Bella. And she started strumming her guitar. "And a one, and a two, and a three, let's go!"

Emily joined in using her shakers and bells. Sam picked up the beat on his drums. And Maddie whisked along on her washboard.

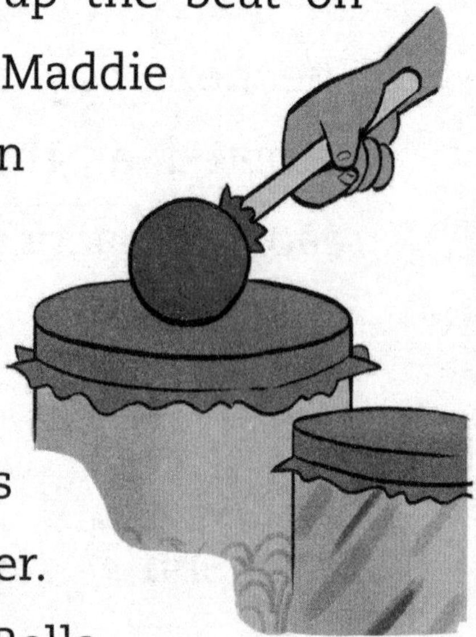

When they got to the end of the song, the friends looked at each other.

"Not bad," said Bella.

"But not *great*," said Emily.

The friends tried a few other songs, but none of them were quite right. Then Bella had an idea.

"Maybe," she said, "we should play something different. Like . . . our own song?"

"How would we do that?" asked Sam.

“Well, in my guitar lessons, we used to improvise sometimes,” Bella said. “Like this: Sam, drop a beat.”

Sam began tapping out a rhythm on his drums.

“Now I’m going to add my guitar.” Bella began strumming, paying attention to Sam’s beat but weaving in her own twangy notes.

"Maddie, you ready to jump in?" Bella asked.

Maddie nodded and began skritch-scratching away.

"Guessing that means it's my turn," said Emily, and she picked up two shakers so she could add two distinct sounds to the song they were forming.

Slowly, smiles came to all four faces.

"We sound . . . not bad!" said Bella. The others nodded in agreement.

"If we keep practicing, we're going to sound great!" said Sam.

And so they practiced for the rest of the afternoon.

By the time Maddie's, Emily's, and Sam's parents came to pick them up, the kids were exhausted.

As Maddie was walking out, she suddenly gasped and turned around. "Guys, we don't have a band name!"

CHAPTER
9

Four Surprises

The day before the talent show, all of Mason Creek Elementary was buzzing with excitement.

To Emily, Maddie, Bella, and Sam, it felt like the longest school day ever. Finally the bell rang. The four friends grabbed their things and practically ran out of the school building.

"Hey, what's that?" asked Emily, noticing Maddie was carrying an extra bag.

"It's a surprise," said Maddie mysteriously.

And when they all arrived at the craft studio, Maddie showed her friends what exactly was in that bag.

She pulled out four black T-shirts. Each one had a band member's name scrawled on the back in silver fabric paint. Maddie had then decorated the backs with patches and buttons and designs out of multicolored threads. Each one was unique.

"These are *so* cool!" Emily exclaimed.

"But there's one thing missing," said Maddie. "There's nothing on the front of the shirts because we haven't picked a band name yet!"

"Fantastic Four?" threw out Sam.

"*Craftastic* Four?" Bella chimed in.

"What about Craftastic *Crew*?" Emily suggested.

At that suggestion, a smile spread across the face of each kid. That was it!

Maddie had brought her silver paint with her. She grabbed brushes from Sam's Painting Pavilion and passed them around so everyone could add their new band name to the custom T-shirts.

“Hey, speaking of painting, I have a surprise too.” Sam pulled out a roll of paper from a long tube he had borrowed from his dad. He unrolled it to display a gorgeous painted backdrop for the band.

“That’s amazing, Sam!” said Emily.

“I left room for the band name,” Sam pointed out. “And I think I have some regular silver paint that would match the T-shirts perfectly!”

“I *also* have a surprise,” said Emily. She went to the back of the shed and pulled out a wooden storage crate to which she had added

wheels and a handle. "This way we can bring our instruments into the auditorium more easily."

"And I borrowed some extra microphones from the music room, plus speakers to rig them up to," said Bella.

"Wow," said Sam, admiring the shirts, the instruments, and the gear. "We make a pretty great team, don't we?"

And it was true. They really did make a good team. But that team also knew they needed just a little more practice.

Following Bella's lead, the kids picked up their instruments and got in position. The talent show was the next night, so it was their last chance to get their sound just right!

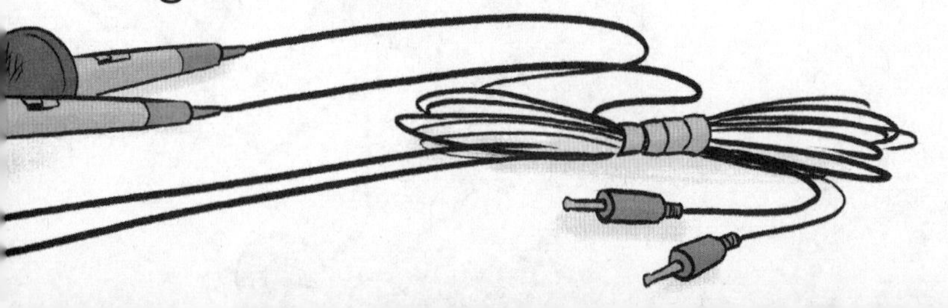

CHAPTER
10

Rock On!

"Good evening! Welcome to the Mason Creek Elementary School talent show."

Principal Park stood at the microphone, beaming. Bella, Maddie, Emily, and Sam waited backstage. They were surrounded by jugglers, gymnasts, singers, dancers, and other talented classmates.

BELLA

Sam tapped his drumsticks nervously. He could hear the audience clapping and laughing as Lyle and Cory did their infamous pulling-a-frog-out-of-a-hat magic trick onstage.

"We're next," said Bella.

Suddenly Maddie gasped. "Where are my whisk and spoon?" she asked frantically.

Everyone searched about, but they were nowhere to be found.

"What am I going to do?" Maddie knew her washboard would work only if she had something to play it with. Meanwhile, the magic act was about to end and they would be going onstage soon! Maddie was close to tears. All that hard work only to have it ruined by a last-minute mix-up.

Bella, who had been digging through her backpack, pulled out two objects and held them out to Maddie. "Try using these instead!"

"Really?" asked Maddie.

Bella shrugged. "What do you have to lose?"

Before Maddie could reply, Lyle and Cory returned triumphantly and the friends heard Principal Park introducing the next act.

"I'm proud to introduce four students who are so creative, they don't just make music. They make their own musical instruments, too! I present to you: the Craftastic Crew."

The big moment had arrived. The four friends marched onstage and set up their instruments.

Sam looked at the others, gave a nod, and began to tap out a beat on his drums.

Tap, tap, tap-tap-tap.

Bella joined in, twanging away at her strings. Emily came in next, adding the rhythm of her various shakers to the mix.

Maddie took a deep breath. "Here goes nothing," she whispered. Then she took the two Brushbots Bella had handed to her and scratched their stiff bristles tentatively across her washboard.

Scritcha-scritcha! Scritcha-scritcha!

The scratchy noise was perfect! Encouraged, she flipped the switches and the Brushbots sprang to life, scrubbing away. She moved them up and down on her washboard, producing a faster scratching sound than before, which sounded great.

Craftastic
The

Then the audience started clapping along!

It's like a real jam session, thought Sam, drumming away excitedly.

The audience really likes our sound, thought Bella. She closed her eyes and imagined herself rocking out in a huge stadium.

When they finished playing, there was a brief moment of silence. Then thunderous applause!

The friends could not stop grinning even after they were backstage.

"We did it!" said Bella, jumping up and down.

That night, even though it had been a long and exhausting day, Bella couldn't seem to fall asleep. She picked up her homemade guitar and plucked its strings, remembering how it felt to perform in front of the whole school with her best friends. It was funny how they'd started with nothing, not even an idea. Then they'd lost everything to a leaky roof. But they didn't give up. They had worked together and—Bella stood on her bed, strummed a chord, and struck a pose—the Craftastic Crew had totally *rocked* the talent show!

How to Make . . .
A Cereal Box Guitar

What you need:

Cereal box
Spaghetti box
Craft knife
Rubber bands
Glue
Corks
Straw
Paints and paintbrush

Step 1:

Paint the boxes any way you like!

Step 2:
Step 3:
Stretch the rubber bands over the middle of the cereal box.

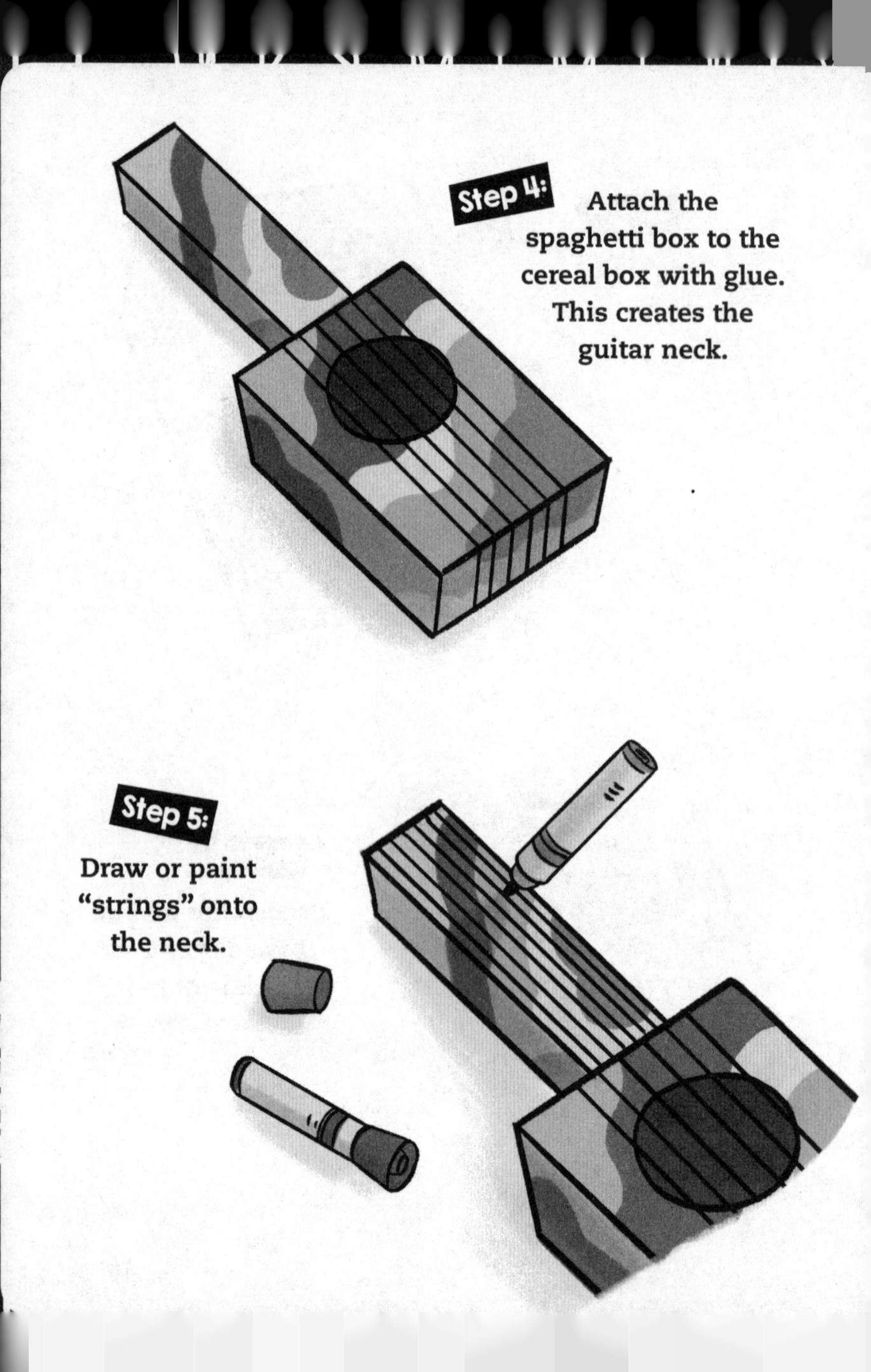
Step 4:
Attach the spaghetti box to the cereal box with glue. This creates the guitar neck.
Step 5:
Draw or paint "strings" onto the neck.

Step 6: Cut holes on the sides of the spaghetti box and insert corks for the pretend tuning keys. Use glue to keep these in place.

Below the hole on the cereal box, glue a straw underneath the rubber bands. This creates the bridge, which will help make a sound when you strum! Now rock on!

Tie-Dye Disaster

SALT
Fabric
Dye

CONTENTS

CHAPTER
1

The Call

Maddie Wilson's slippered feet swung back and forth under her bedroom desk. *Scratch*, *scratch* went her pencil. This dress had a sweetheart neckline and feathers all over the skirt. Maddie got some of her best ideas first thing in the morning.

She was just adding the final touches to her latest design sketch when a familiar, mouthwatering smell reached her. "*Mmmmmmm!* Pancakes!"

Maddie ran downstairs. "Thanks so much, Mom! You make the best—"

"Sorry, kiddo," said Maddie's father, standing at the stove and

waving his spatula. "Your regular pancake maker is not available this morning. Luckily, she's not the only one who can flip a flapjack around here."

"Sorry, Dad!" said Maddie. "Where is Mom?"

"In her sewing studio. This is

a busy time of year, so she's been there since sunup. You should go say good morning. But first—get 'em while they're hot!" he said, handing her a plate. Maddie did not need to be told twice.

When she finished eating, she volunteered to bring breakfast to her mom.

“Thanks, sweetie,” said Margie Wilson, looking up from her sewing machine. “Hey, do you have time to give me some feedback on my designs? I need someone with a critical eye and a passion for fashion.”

"Sure!" said Maddie. It was fun to have a mom who was a seamstress. Maddie thoughtfully studied several pencil sketches with swatches of fabric taped to them. "Hmmm . . . that dress would look amazing if you added some sequins

to the hemline. And maybe using a brighter color, like coral, would make it pop—"

Just then Maddie's dad burst in, holding out a phone.

"It's him!" he whispered urgently.

Maddie's mom quickly grabbed the phone. There were a lot of "Yes, sirs" and "Thank you, sirs." Then, "Oh! So soon!" and finally, "You can count on me, sir."

She hung up and sank back in her chair.

"I still can't believe he hired me," she said.

"Who?" asked Maddie.

"Mayor Barnstable," explained Maddie's mom. "He asked me to create a custom-tailored suit for him to wear to the unveiling of the new town hall."

"Wow!" said Maddie. "That's huge."

"Huge and terrifying," said Maddie's mom. "I just learned that the big event is Saturday night. That's less than a week away!"

"You can do it, Mom!" Maddie said confidently. Suddenly, she had a thought: *Wow! This could make Mom famous! And if she gets famous . . . will that make me famous?*

CHAPTER
2

Some Colorful Inspiration

That night, Maddie drifted off to sleep still thinking about her mother's important new client. She wondered if mayors had red carpets, like movie stars. She pictured reporters and photographers begging the mayor for details about his fabulous outfit.

"My designer? Of course it's

Maddie and Margie Wilson. They're the best in town."

Maddie imagined boarding a private airplane with her mom, rushing off to help dress someone fabulous. What a team they'd be, traveling the world. And all the stars begging, "*Maddie, you must design for me. Please, Maddie! Maddie?*"

"Maddie?"

"Huh?" Maddie opened one eye.

"That must have been some dream," said her dad. He was standing in her bedroom doorway. "I've been calling your name for a while. It's time to get up for school."

Maddie arrived in class just as the bell rang. She slid into her seat and grinned at her best friends, Emily Adams, Bella Diaz, and Sam Sharma. Boy, was she excited to tell them about yesterday's big call!

But before Maddie could whisper her good news, their teacher,

Ms. Gibbons, cleared her throat to get the class's attention.

Guess I'll have to wait till recess, Maddie thought, disappointed.

"We're starting a new unit today," announced Ms. Gibbons. "The next decade we're going to study is, well, *groovy*, as they used to say. Welcome to the 1960s!"

She showed images, played music, and told the class about all the things that had changed in the course of just a few years.

"Politics, opinions, laws . . . music, too. A popular sixties song was about how 'the times, they are a-changing.' That was definitely true," she explained. "And

the clothes changed a lot too—some of the styles, well, they were pretty out there."

The classroom exploded with laughter at some of the outrageous clothing Ms. Gibbons showed on the screen. Jeans with giant flared "bell" bottoms. Dresses in neon colors and crazy patterns. Jackets with wings of suede fringe and beaded peace signs. But

other fashion trends looked surprisingly familiar.

"Hey!" said Cory. "I have a shirt just like that!"

Ms. Gibbons smiled. "That's tie-dye. It was very popular in the sixties."

"Cool!" said Maddie, practically bouncing in

her seat. Ms. Gibbons's presentation had given her a great idea. Now she had *two* exciting things to tell her friends!

At recess, Maddie's friends were as impressed by her news as she hoped they would be.

"Are you going to meet the mayor? Can *we* meet the mayor?" asked Emily.

"Maybe," said Maddie. "Oh, and I have an idea for our next crafting project!" The four friends met regularly to do crafts at their craft clubhouse—otherwise known as the old shed they had fixed up in Bella's yard. "How about we tie-dye?"

"You know how to tie-dye?" asked Sam.

"Sure!" said Maddie. "My mom taught me. You just bind cloth with rubber bands or string and dip it into dye. Where the fabric is covered, the dye can't reach, so you get a pattern."

They all started talking excitedly, and soon it was decided: They would each collect old white clothing and fabric scraps at home and meet at the clubhouse the next day after school.

CHAPTER
3

On the Hunt

“Today’s your lucky day,” said Emily’s mom when she asked about possible items to tie-dye. “I was just weeding out some old things.” She pointed to a pile of clothing. “Take whatever you’d like.” Emily found two of her dad’s old white T-shirts. One had a lot of holes, but the other was just right.

"Perfect!" she said.

Sam, however, quickly discovered a problem: His artistic family favored bright clothing. He could not find *anything* light-colored except . . .

"Can you tie-dye socks?" Sam asked.

“Maybe. You could also try this,” said his dad, holding up a length of thick fabric. “It’s an old painting drop cloth, so there’s some paint on it, but I still think it could end up looking pretty cool.”

“You mean *groovy*,” Sam corrected his dad.

Maddie dug around in her closet until she found an old white dress. She had worn it almost every day last summer . . . until she had accidentally squirted ketchup all down the front mid–hot dog bite.

Maybe I can hide the stain under some colorful dye, Maddie thought.

She went to her mom's sewing room to get a second opinion. When Maddie explained her idea, her mom smiled.

"So resourceful," she said. "And so smart to recycle and refresh!"

"Speaking of fresh," said Maddie, "did you come up with a fresh idea for the mayor's outfit?"

"See for yourself." She pointed to her bulletin board.

"Oh," said Maddie, not sure what else to say. The sketch looked like . . . a basic, regular suit.

"I decided to go with a solid navy," continued her mom. "I think it will look really sharp in pictures."

Maddie knew that her mom had

a good point. And she did think the suit looked sharp. But she couldn't help feeling worried for her mom.

The suit might photograph well, but it was also pretty boring! There had to be some way to jazz it up. "What if you took some funky buttons and—"

"I'm sorry, honey," her mom interrupted, "but I just don't have the time to really fiddle around with things. I've already purchased everything I need, and with only four more days, time is of the essence!"

Maddie nodded. She didn't want to make her mom worry or slow her down. Margie Wilson already looked stressed enough!

"Looks awesome," Maddie finally said.

She felt a small pang of sadness that her mom didn't have time to even hear her idea, but her mom knew what was best. Right?

CHAPTER
4

Maddie the Resourceful

The next day, the four friends met up at Bella's house. They went straight to the clubhouse and dumped their fabric finds on the big worktable.

"*Socks?*" Emily held one up, raising an eyebrow.

"And a drop cloth!" Sam added.

"I couldn't find anything," Bella apologized. "My parents donated a bunch of our old things right before we moved."

"It's okay," said Sam. "We can share my socks. I'll take the right one. You take the left!"

The friends laughed. Then Maddie got a better idea. "Hey, my mom has tons of extra fabric in her sewing studio! I'll run home and look while you guys set up."

After Maddie left, the others got to work. Emily gathered buckets, stirring sticks, and rubber bands. She also spread out newspapers to protect the worktable. Then Sam prepared the dye. "How about primary colors?" he asked. "Red, blue, and of course—"

"Yellow!" chorused Emily and Bella, giggling. It was Sam's favorite color.

Bella used her computer to research and print out an article on tie-dyeing that included instructions and designs. Spirals, bull's-eyes, stripes, rosettes—there were so many good options!

Meanwhile, Maddie arrived home and discovered that her mom was out running errands. She hesitated before going to the sewing studio.

Maybe I should wait until Mom comes back? she thought.

But then Maddie remembered what her mother had said about the tie-dye project in the first place: “So resourceful!” Maddie smiled, thinking of how fun it would be to surprise her mom by showing just how resourceful she could be. Besides, her mom had been so busy earlier. There was no way she would have time to help sort through scraps. Maddie had assisted in the sewing room so many times, she was sure she could figure out which odds and ends were up for grabs.

In a corner by the door, Maddie spied a shopping bag. Perfect! She grabbed the bag and quickly started filling it with fabric scraps. She also dumped her mom's rag basket out

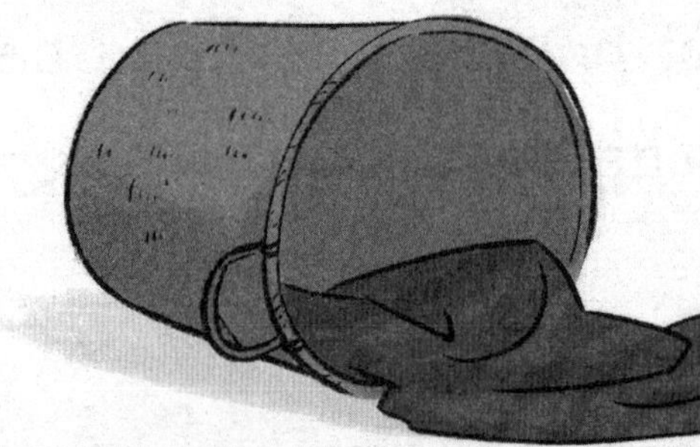

and found some old clothing items that she knew her mother would not mind her taking. She would return the bag and any scraps they didn't use later, but now she had plenty for Bella to choose from!

On her way out of the room, the drawing of the mayor's suit caught her eye.

Did he ask for a boring suit? she wondered. She really hoped so, because it looked like that was exactly what he was going to get.

"Oh good, you're back!" Sam said to Maddie. He and Emily were stirring buckets of dye. "Now all we need is—"

"Who ordered the salt?" sang Bella, returning from the kitchen.

"How did you know to add salt?" asked Maddie. Her mom had taught her that salt was the secret to making colors even brighter.

Bella pointed at the computer.

"Aha, I should have known!" said Maddie.

The rest of the afternoon flew by as the four friends pinched and twisted fabric, wrapped and rewrapped rubber bands, and dipped and dunked their creations into buckets of dye. At first they stuck to the designs they had read about, but then they began to experiment. What would happen if they did a bunch of rosettes in a pattern, like a heart or a star? What if they did two spirals on the same piece of fabric, but in different spots? They also combined some of the colors of dye. Now they had green, orange, and purple, too!

That night at dinner, the phone rang. Maddie raised an eyebrow.

The Wilson family didn't usually get calls this late. But when Maddie's mom saw who was calling, she excused herself from the table, grabbed the phone, and stepped into the hall. Maddie could only hear snippets of the conversation.

"Okay, off-white, silk, French cuffs . . . ," she heard her mom say. "I feel like I saw it in the bag, but I

thought I had emptied it. . . . Yes, sir, I'll double-check, of course. And if you find it, your office can send it over anytime. . . . Thank *you*, sir!"

Maddie's mom hung up the phone and walked down the hall. When she returned to the kitchen a few minutes later, she looked puzzled.

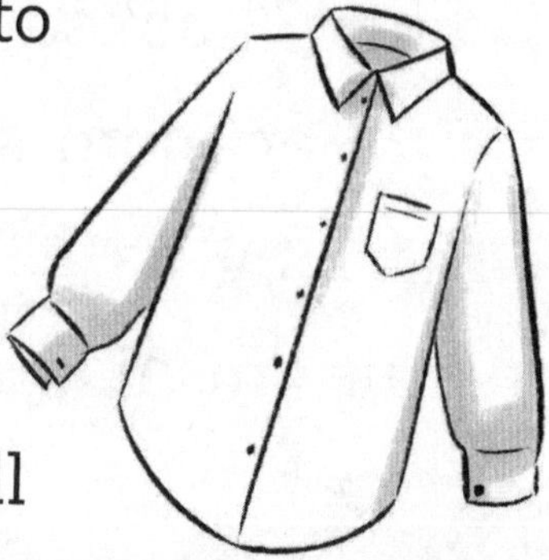

"What was that all about?" asked Maddie's dad.

"Oh, the mayor has a special shirt he wants to wear with the suit I'm making. There's been a bit of a mix-up, though. His office was supposed to send it to me, but I just double-checked the sewing room and I don't have it. And, apparently, neither does he."

"Can't he just wear another shirt?" asked Maddie.

Her mom shrugged. "Of course, as long as it goes with the suit I'm making."

Maddie felt a stomach pang—and it had nothing to do with how hungry she was. She wanted to tell her mom what she really thought about the suit, but she couldn't think of a nice way to do it. Her mom always said, "If you can't say something nice, maybe you shouldn't say anything at all."

CHAPTER
5

The Magical Mystery Shirt

The next day, when school let out, Maddie and her friends couldn't get to the clubhouse fast enough. They had left all their creations tightly bound overnight so the colors could fully sink in. Now it was time for the big reveal.

First, Emily grabbed her dad's old T-shirt and snipped the rubber bands, being careful not to nip the fabric in the process. She unrolled it and . . .

Everybody gasped.

"Wow!" said Sam. "It's like a sunset, only brighter!"

Maddie unwrapped the stained dress next. It was now bright blue with purple rosettes forming a peace sign. The design completely hid the ketchup stain!

Then Bella unraveled a shirt that was more colorful than all the others. With its silky fabric, it looked like a shimmering rainbow.

"That one turned out so cool," said Maddie. "Who brought it?"

"Not me," said Emily. "I just brought the T-shirt."

"I just brought a drop cloth," said Sam.

"And socks! Don't forget the socks," joked Emily.

"There wasn't anything from my house," said Bella. "That's why you went home to get more stuff, remember?"

"It looks like a man's shirt," said Sam. "Maybe it's your dad's, Maddie?"

"I don't think so . . . ," said Maddie, trying to recall what she had brought. She had gathered up everything so fast, she wasn't entirely sure what ended up in the bag. It didn't look like something her dad would wear, though.

"Well, it's a magical mystery shirt, I guess," said Sam. "But I like it. If your dad doesn't claim it, I'll definitely wear it!"

The others laughed, including Maddie. Then Sam revealed his pair of mismatched tie-dyed socks, which made them laugh harder.

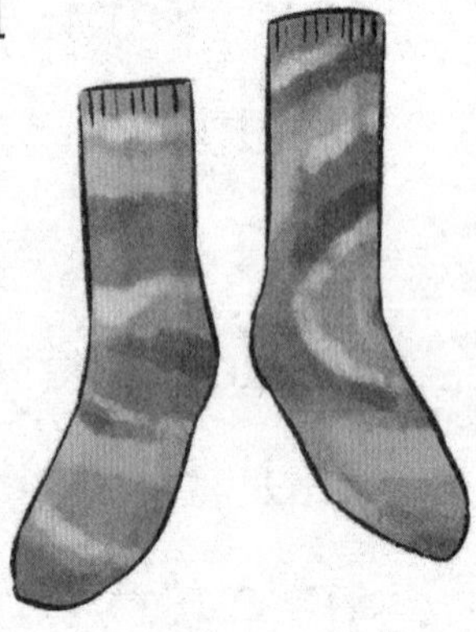

As Bella started to hang up the mystery shirt to dry, she noticed something. "Hey, a clue!" she said. "Look at the cuff."

The others followed her gaze.

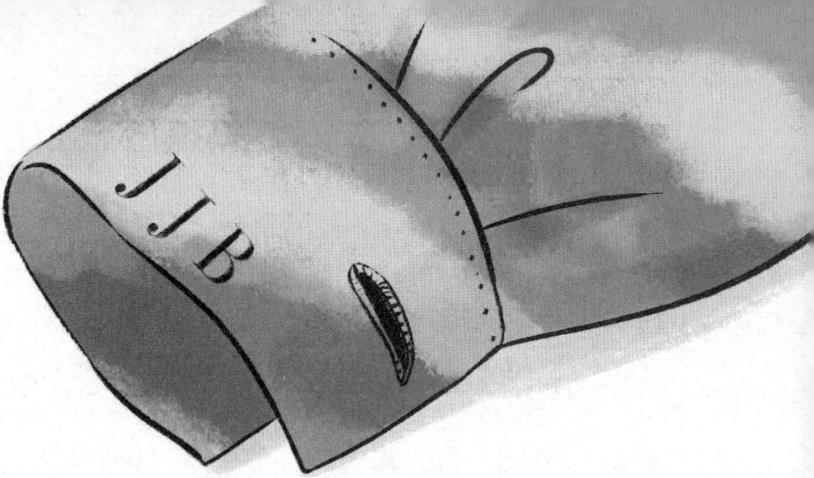

"'JJB,'" read Sam. "What is JJB?"

"You mean *who* is JJB," said Bella. "It's a monogram. Those are probably the initials of whoever owns this shirt."

"My dad's initials are RPW," said Maddie, "so it definitely isn't . . ."

Her voice trailed off as she suddenly had an awful thought. *Oh no. It couldn't be.*

"Bella, can you go online and do a search for Mayor Barnstable?" Maddie asked.

"Sure." Bella typed and clicked, then said, "Got it. Mayor James J. Barnstable's website. What do you want to know?"

"I couldn't . . . ," said Maddie. "I didn't . . ."

Her friends looked at her, confused. She almost couldn't say it.

"James J. Barnstable," she finally said. "JJB. I tie-dyed the mayor's shirt."

CHAPTER
6

How Do You Un-Tie-Dye?

"What?" said Emily. "That's not possible."

"Why did you have the mayor's shirt?" asked Bella.

"His office sent it to my mom because she's designing that suit for him. It must have been in the shopping bag I grabbed. I thought it was empty!" Maddie was close to tears. "I didn't mean to take it. And I certainly didn't mean to tie-dye it!"

Emily patted Maddie on the back. "It was a mistake. It will be okay," she said.

"No, it won't," said Maddie. "Because it gets worse! This is the special shirt he was going to wear with his new suit for the big event. What am I going to do?"

"You mean what are *we* going going to do?" said Sam. "We tie-dyed the shirt together, so we're going to fix it together."

"How?" asked Maddie. "You can't *un*-tie-dye a shirt."

"Are you sure?" asked Bella. "My dad's a chef, remember? I've seen a *lot* of food stains. There are all sorts of ways to get stains out of clothing, so why not dye?"

"Really?" asked Emily. "Like what?"

"Well, the worst stain was mole sauce. It's a Mexican sauce made with chili pepper and chocolate, so it was pretty bad."

"As bad as dye?" asked Maddie. "You may have been able to get chocolate out, but how are we going to get the dye out?"

"Let's see!" Bella turned her attention back to the computer screen. "Looks like one method we could try is using laundry detergent, baking soda, and white vinegar. I'm pretty sure we have everything we need."

Bella dashed over to her house and back again.

"Good news," she reported. "My

dad must really like vinegar. We had balsamic vinegar, red wine vinegar, cider vinegar . . . practically every vinegar under the sun, including *white* vinegar!" And with that, Bella plopped down a big glass bottle.

Bella sat back down at her computer to read the instructions. "Okay, you're supposed to soak the shirt in

vinegar," she said. "Then you make a paste out of baking soda and more vinegar and rub that on the stain. Then you wash the shirt with detergent and even *more* vinegar."

"Good thing it's a full bottle," said Emily.

The four friends carefully followed the instructions. When they got to the final step, Maddie rinsed the shirt with cold water until all the bubbles were gone.

"Hey, I think it's working," said Sam, pointing to the colored water filling the sink.

"You do?" Maddie held up the wet shirt.

She wished she could agree. The colors might have faded a little, but the shirt still looked like a rainbow. Maddie leaned in to take a closer look. "Ewww!" she said, recoiling in

horror. "Now it reeks of vinegar, too!"

"Okay, don't panic," said Emily. "Let's try something else. What if instead of trying to remove the colors, we added more color? That way at least it would be one color, not lots of them."

"We *could* . . . ," said Sam thoughtfully. "But too many colors mixed together usually just makes brown. Do you think the suit your mom designed would look good with a brown shirt?" he asked Maddie.

Maddie groaned in response. *How can things have gotten so messed up?* she thought. Maddie might not have been a huge fan of the suit her mom designed, but she certainly didn't want to make it worse!

"Don't worry, Maddie," said Bella.

"We'll figure something out."

"Totally," agreed Emily.

Maddie nodded glumly. She hoped her friends were right.

They had to find a way out of this tie-dye disaster, and fast. The mayor's big event was only a few days away!

CHAPTER
7

Looking for a Sign

At bedtime, Maddie turned out her light and tried to sleep. But in her head she saw herself holding up the shirt and seeing the horrified look on the mayor's face.

Poof! went the private plane. *Poof!* went the parties, the premieres, and Maddie's future as a famous fashion designer.

And what about her mom? What if the mayor was angry—like, *really* angry?

"You'll never work in this town again!" she heard him say to her mom. "You're out. You all have to go!"

"But—but—" sputtered Maddie. Her mom and dad were standing there with suitcases, so she knew there was nothing she could say.

She ran to tell Emily, Bella, and Sam. But as she did, they turned away. Clearly, they wanted nothing to do with her.

"I'm so sorry! Please don't make us move!" Maddie begged the mayor. "I like my friends. I like my town."

But the mayor wasn't listening. Or maybe he couldn't hear her? The

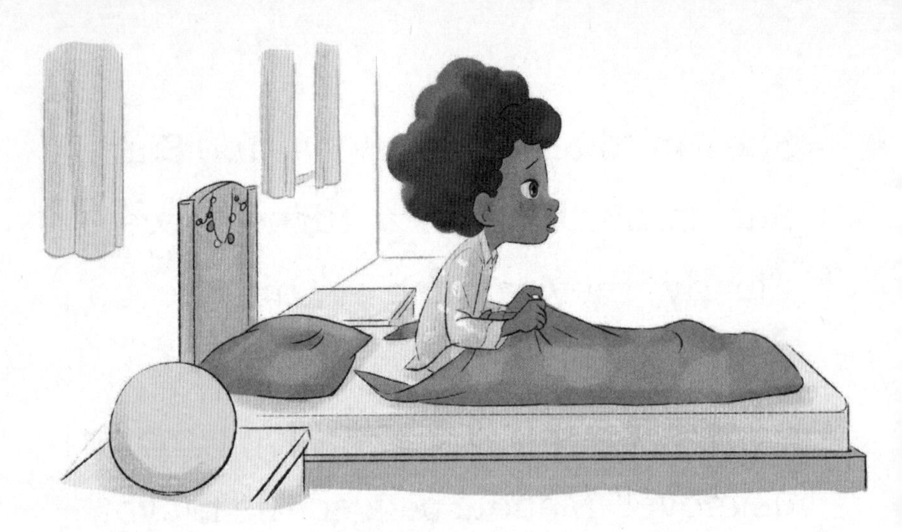

new town seemed really loud—

Maddie sat up abruptly. She looked around and then flopped back in relief. It had all been a bad dream: the mean mayor, the loud new town. *Maybe I even dreamed the part about the tie-dye disaster,* she thought hopefully. She got up and peeked into her backpack.

Nope, that part was real. In her backpack was a ziplock bag containing the damp rainbow fabric formerly known as the mayor's special silk shirt.

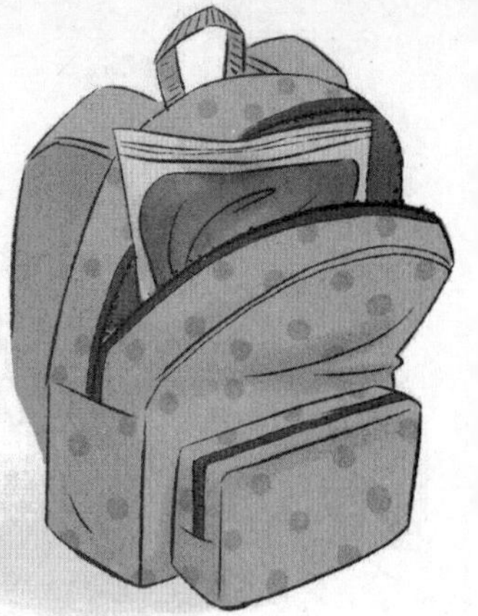

The other thing from her dream that was real was the noise. Maddie went downstairs and found her father vacuuming and her mother cranking her favorite cleaning-the-house music.

Maddie's dad turned off the vacuum when he noticed Maddie. "Morning, sweetie."

"Sorry if we woke you," said Maddie's mom. "Just trying to get this place pulled together. We have a special visitor coming this afternoon: the mayor himself!"

On her way to school, Maddie was quiet. She kept trying to think of a way to tell her mom about the mayor's shirt. But every time she opened her mouth, she closed it again. Her mom was so excited to have such an important opportunity. How could Maddie ruin it?

At recess, Maddie quickly quizzed her friends on possible solutions.

"I looked online, and I even asked my dad. Don't worry—I didn't tell him why," said Bella. "But all I could find used bleach, which is a bad idea."

"Why?" asked Sam. "Bleach makes things white, right?"

"Yes," said Bella. "But it is also

strong enough to burn holes in delicate fabrics."

"Like a silk shirt," said Maddie glumly.

"I've been thinking about this," said Emily. "How about we go with you to tell your mom?" Sam and Bella both nodded.

Maddie smiled gratefully at her friends. "You guys are the best," she said. "But I was the one who made the mistake in the first place. I should probably be the one to take responsibility for it."

As the day went on, Maddie

tried hard to build up her confidence for the difficult task she faced. She looked for signs of support everywhere, and happily she found them. First, from her friends, who promised to come along if she changed her mind. Next, from the cafeteria, where her favorite lunch—pizza!—was being served, even though it was supposed to be meat loaf day.

Then she got her spelling test back. At the top of the page was "Great Job!" and a rainbow peace sign sticker. Rainbow, like the mayor's shirt, and peace. Maybe the mayor would be . . . peaceful when he realized his outfit was ruined. Maddie was finally ready to tell her mom about the tie-dye disaster.

She *thought* she was ready. That is, until her dad brought her home from school. There were two unfamiliar cars in the driveway and another car parked in front of the house.

"Wow, looks like he's here already!" said Maddie's dad.

The mayor had arrived.

CHAPTER
8

Smells Like Disaster

Maddie wanted to run.

Maddie wanted to hide.

Maddie wanted to do anything but walk through her front door and meet the mayor.

But there was no way out. Before she could think of a plan or an excuse or anything, Maddie found herself in the entryway and her

mom saying, “Mr. Mayor, I’d like you to meet my husband, Robert, and our daughter, Maddie.”

Maddie watched as her father shook hands with the mayor. Then he extended his hand to her. Maddie just stared.

“Maddie?” said her mom.

Maddie blinked and snapped herself out of it. The mayor smiled reassuringly as he shook her hand. “It’s so great to meet you, Maddie. Your mom has been telling me that you are as good a designer as she is—which is saying a lot! She also says you're the most creative member of the family!"

"Would you like a photo with the mayor?" asked one of the official-looking people standing in Maddie's front hall. He motioned to a woman with a camera.

Maddie stood frozen, her backpack still on one shoulder, as the mayor got in position right next to Maddie. Her parents, standing behind the photographer, beamed, which made Maddie realize she wasn't even smiling.

"Thanks," the mayor said to

Maddie. "It is not often that I get to meet such a talented young artist like yourself." He pointed to her backpack. "Any chance you have any works of art in there I could see?"

"Oh, I, uh . . . ," stammered Maddie.

"Maddie, don't be shy," her mother said.

"She's always sketching out her ideas," said her dad.

"I mean, I . . ." Maddie unzipped her backpack slowly, hoping she'd quickly come across her drawing pad or something. But the moment she opened her bag, she regretted it.

"Whew!" said the mayor. He scrunched up his nose and stepped back quickly. "What is that powerful smell?"

"Oh no! I . . ." Maddie panicked. She dropped her backpack like a hot potato. It tipped over and out fell the bag with the rainbow shirt in it.

"Maddie, what on earth?" asked her father.

Her mother picked up the bag by one corner and sniffed it.

"It's . . . it's . . ." Maddie took a deep breath. A million possible answers ran through her head, but only one was right.

She summoned all her courage and looked the mayor in the eye.

"I'm so sorry, Mr. Mayor, sir," she said. "It's your shirt."

CHAPTER
9

Feeling Groovy

Maddie couldn't bear to look at her mom. Instead she stared hard at the mayor's shoes. Suddenly, something strange happened. The mayor started to chuckle. When Maddie looked up, he had a funny look on his face that confused her.

The mayor seemed to be . . . smiling?

"May I see my shirt?" he asked.

Maddie nodded slowly. Her mom opened the plastic bag, removed the damp shirt, and held it up.

"Did you . . . tie-dye it?" the mayor asked.

Maddie nodded again, then closed her eyes tightly. She wanted to disappear.

The mayor started laughing even harder. "It's completely brilliant!" he said.

Maddie's eyes snapped open. "You *like* it?"

Now it was the mayor's turn to nod. "My dear," he said, "I am a

child of the 1960s. So naturally, I love tie-dye. Being the mayor, of course, I don't get to wear it every day. But it's not every day that we unveil the new town hall. It's a very special event and it deserves a very special shirt, don't you think?"

"Yes . . . sir," said Maddie, shocked.

"When I hired your mother, I knew she would find a way to wow me. My team told me she had a reputation for creating classic, elegant designs with an unexpected flair. Put this shirt together with the suit your mother has sewn and that's exactly what we'll have! A classic, elegant suit and a shirt with an unexpected flair!"

Maddie was still shocked. But she felt something else, too. She felt relief. Her mom wasn't going to lose her job! Maybe there would be private jets and celebrity clients in her future after all!

"Sir, I promise we'll have it

pressed and smelling fresh as roses by tomorrow," Maddie's mom said. "And I think I know the perfect way to tie it in with the rest of your outfit!"

After the mayor left, Maddie knew there was still one thing she had to do.

"Mom, I'm *so* sorry," she said. Then she explained everything: how she hadn't wanted Bella to feel left out. How she'd grabbed the empty shopping bag to carry the fabric scraps

and hadn't noticed the mayor's shirt at the bottom. How she and her friends had tried really, really hard to fix it.

When Maddie finished, she could tell that her mother was disappointed.

"I don't ever want you to take something from my sewing studio without permission again," said Mrs. Wilson. "Do you understand?"

"Yes, ma'am," said Maddie. And she meant it.

Then, to Maddie's surprise, her mother swept her into a big hug. It felt great, but Maddie had to ask, "What was that for?"

"For saving the day, sweetie," replied her mom.

"I saved the day?" Maddie asked.

"Yup." Her mom smiled and explained. "I worked hard on my design, and I am proud of it, but I kept feeling like there was something missing. Now I know exactly what it needed: you! I should have listened when you tried to help the other day."

Maddie couldn't believe it. She beamed with pride.

She was so excited to tell her friends how everything had worked out. But that would have to wait until school the next day. She and her mom still had important work to do!

After dinner, she joined her mom in the sewing studio. Maddie sewed a pocket square made from one of

the tie-dyed fabric scraps to match the mayor's radical shirt. Her mom put the finishing touches on what turned out to be an extremely elegant—and not at all boring—suit. She even added funky buttons sewn on with different-colored thread to tie everything together. Then they thoroughly washed the mayor's shirt (twice), pressed everything, and set it out on hangers.

Maddie and her mom stood back to admire their work.

"I must say, the outfit turned out perfect," said Mrs. Wilson. "The mayor is going to look really great."

"And really groovy," added Maddie with a smile.

CHAPTER
10

Making Headlines

A few days later, Maddie woke up to a familiar, delicious smell.

She grabbed her bathrobe and ran downstairs.

There was her mom, flipping the flapjacks. There was her dad, sitting at the table.

And there were her friends, Bella, Emily, and Sam, joining them for breakfast.

"Surprise!" said Maddie's dad. "We invited your friends over for a special celebration breakfast in honor of last night's success!"

"I brought homemade whipped cream!" said Bella.

"And chocolate syrup," added Sam.

"And sliced strawberries!" said Emily.

"Wait, *success?*" Maddie asked her mom. "You mean the mayor's gala went well? The outfit was a hit? Tell me everything!"

"See for yourself." Maddie's mom pointed to the newspaper.

"Wow!" said Maddie. "Look, it's the mayor in his new outfit! The one you made!"

"The one we all made," her mom corrected her, smiling at the kids around the table. Maddie had told her mom that even though the mistake of taking the mayor's shirt was all *hers*, the tie-dying—as well as the attempts to *fix* the tie-dye disaster—had been a team effort.

"And check *this* out," Maddie's dad said, pointing to the writing beneath the photo.

MAYOR BARNSTABLE CELEBRATES AT LAST NIGHT'S GALA FOR THE NEW TOWN HALL. HIS FESTIVE ENSEMBLE WAS CREATED BY LOCAL SEAMSTRESS MARGARET WILSON, WITH SPECIAL HELP FROM HER DAUGHTER, MADDIE WILSON.

How to Make . . .
A Tie-Dye Shirt

What you need:

Fabric dye
3-gallon enamel or stainless-steel containers
(You can use plastic, but it will get stained.)
1 cup of salt
Rubber bands
Tongs
Long-handled spoon
Fork
White cotton shirt or other
clothing item of your choice

In a container, mix fabric dye according to the instructions on the package.

Step 2:

Add a cup of salt to the dye bath to brighten the color.

Step 3:

To make a spiral, lay the T-shirt flat. Holding a fork in the center of the shirt, twist clockwise.

Gather the shirt into a circle and wrap 4 to 6 rubber bands around the shirt in a rough star shape.

Take your rubber-banded T-shirt and immerse in hot water. Wring out excess water and then soak in the dye bath.

tir frequently with a long-handled spoon for 10 to 30 minutes (depending on how deep a color you want).

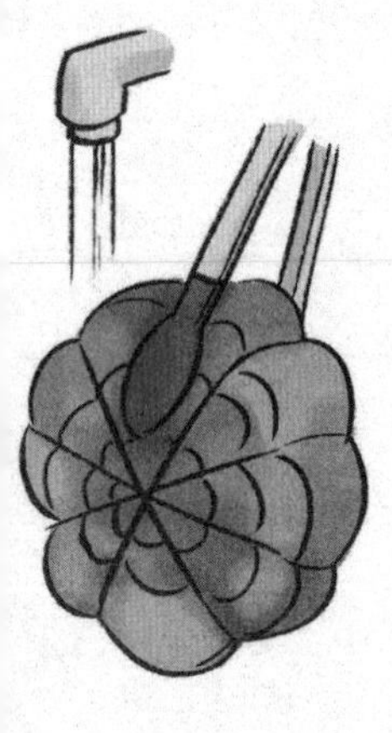

Remove shirt with tongs and rinse under warm water, followed by cooler water until the dye stops bleeding.

Unwrap the T-shirt and line-dry. Ta-da! It's tie-dyed!

Dream Machine

CONTENTS

CHAPTER
1

What a Dream!

Rrrrrrrrrrrr . . .

Bella Diaz stepped on the gas. The engine roared and the race car zoomed forward.

Beaming happily, Bella adjusted a knob on the dashboard. She had designed and programmed the race car herself! Bella loved anything to do with computers: programming, coding, and beyond. And she'd always dreamed of being able to program her very own race car!

She gripped the steering wheel with her purple leather racing gloves as she sped down the race track and into a tight turn.

Just then a light flashed red. *Warning! Warning!*

Oh no! She had taken the turn a little too fast. Bella spun the wheel, leaned hard, and . . .

THUMP!

Bella opened her eyes. She was on the floor next to her bed, twisted up in her blankets.

For a moment she was completely confused. Then she realized what had happened.

Whew, what a dream! Her heart was still racing, thinking about flying around the track. And thinking about that amazing car.

She untangled herself and stood up. Glancing at her alarm clock, she saw that it was still early.

Well, I might as well get up, thought Bella. *I could grab a few more minutes of sleep, but there's no way I'd have a dream that awesome again!*

CHAPTER
2

Robots or Race Cars?

That morning Bella was the first to arrive in Ms. Gibbons's classroom. Still thinking about her dream, she pulled out a notebook. She began sketching a picture of her race car. She wanted to capture all the details before the dream faded.

"Cool car!"

Bella looked up. Her friend Emily

Adams was leaning over the edge of her desk, trying to get a better look at Bella's drawing.

"Thanks," Bella replied. "Last night I dreamed I was driving it. But it was also sort of driving itself because I wrote the code so it would follow the race course. Only I might have miscalculated the turning axis, because—"

"Whoa, whoa, whoa." Emily held up a hand. "Slow down, Bella. You're light-years ahead of me when it comes to programming. Though, if you want some help with the engineering, I'm game. There are some pretty simple things you can do to make the car go faster. Like tapering the back, or adding a spoiler."

Bella grinned. “When I do build my dream car, I’ll definitely want you on the design team.”

“What design team?” asked their friend Sam Sharma, who had just arrived. Sam loved to paint and draw. Clearly, the word “design” had gotten his attention.

Before Bella could explain, the bell rang. There was a sparkly purple blur in the classroom doorway as Maddie Wilson dashed in. She was wearing a sequined dress that Bella was pretty sure had been pink the day before.

Bella smiled. Leave it to Maddie to reinvent her outfit overnight!

Maddie slid into her seat, turned

to her three best friends, and whispered, "What did I miss?"

"We'll tell you at lunch," answered Bella, Emily, and Sam at once.

Over sandwiches, Bella showed Sam and Maddie her race car sketch.

"It's from my dream last night," she explained. "I was thinking maybe it could be the inspiration for our next project!"

The four friends met regularly to do craft projects together, and they were always on the lookout for new ideas.

DISTRICT-WIDE
ROBOT-BUILDING
CONTEST!
DAN
5

Just then two older girls walked by. They were carrying stacks of neon green flyers. But it wasn't just the color that caught Bella's eye; it was the picture of a robot! If there was anything Bella loved more than the idea of programming a race car, it was robots!

Bella watched the girls go from table to table, passing them out. She couldn't wait until the girls got to their table.

But by the time the bell rang, no flyer. And the girls had already left the cafeteria.

Bella was disappointed. What was the robot flyer for? And why did the older girls skip their table? None of her friends seemed to notice—they were still discussing different types of cars they could build.

On the way back to their classroom, a flash of neon green caught Bella's eye. A flyer! It was taped to the wall above a drinking fountain. Bella read it quickly.

Interested? You bet I am, thought Bella.

CHAPTER
3
DISTRICT-WIDE
ROBOT-BUILDING
CONTEST!
Mason Creek Elementary
will be entering a team!
All interested students should
meeting at lunch tomorrow!

The Robotics Team

When the bell rang for lunch the next day, Bella told her friends to go ahead without her. She thought about inviting them to come to the meeting with her. But she decided to check it out herself. If it turned out to be as awesome as she hoped, she could always recruit them later.

Bella found the meeting room.

In her enthusiasm, she threw the door open with a *BANG!*

All eyes turned toward her. There were about ten kids there already, including the two girls who were handing out the flyers. One of them gave Bella a funny look.

"Are you lost?" the girl asked in a tone that made Bella feel like she was about five years old.

"I . . . I don't think so," said Bella, now nervous. "Is this the robotics club?"

A tall, skinny boy laughed. "It's not a *club*. It's a team," he corrected her.

CALENDAR

"That's . . . uh . . . that's what I meant," stammered Bella.

"You can't join. You're too young," said the girl who had asked if Bella was lost.

"Yeah, no little kids allowed," added the tall boy.

"Oh . . . okay," said Bella, completely embarrassed. She turned around to leave. But then she stopped herself. She *really* wanted to know more about this robot-building contest.

Bella turned back around and took a deep breath. "But . . . the poster said *all interested students*," she managed to say.

"Bryce? Naomi? She has a point," said someone from the back of the room. Bella looked and saw that there was a teacher there.

"The rules state that the contest is *recommended* for students ages ten to twelve, but that's only a guideline. So, it's not against the rules for younger students to participate."

"But, Mrs. Jacobs . . . ," complained Naomi.

The teacher held up a hand. "Let's not waste time arguing. We have a lot to get done. Naomi and Bryce, as team captains, will you please explain the rules of the contest?"

Bella felt her heart racing as the two older students rattled off the rules of the robot-building contest. She saw some of the other kids taking notes, so she pulled out her notebook and did the same.

When they got to the end of the rules, Mrs. Jacobs asked, "Any questions?"

Several hands shot up.

"Are they going to provide us with a field set-up kit?"

"Can we use a smartphone as the controller?"

"Is there a limit to how many team members can be in the pit?"

Bella's eyes widened. It seemed like everyone had been on a robotics team before. Everyone except her.

Finally the meeting ended. As Bella put her notebook away, she couldn't help noticing a couple of the kids whispering. Were they talking about her?

Bella sighed. She trudged back to her classroom, feeling defeated. Maybe she should have just walked away the first time.

CHAPTER
4

Second Chances

When school let out, Bella went home, changed her clothes, and then went to wait for her friends at the craft clubhouse in her backyard. As soon as Sam, Maddie, and Emily arrived, the four of them fell into their familiar habit of joking, laughing, and sharing new craft project ideas.

Bella smiled. It felt *so* much better to be at *this* meeting.

"Where were you at lunch, Bella?" asked Maddie. "We came up with the best idea and you totally missed it."

Bella hesitated. Did she even

want to tell her friends about her embarrassing experience with the robotics team? She settled on a shortened version of the story and just told her friends that she'd seen the flyer about a robotics team so she'd gone to check it out.

"There's a robotics team?" asked Emily. "Are you going to join?"

"Probably not," said Bella breezily. "Anyway, what's our idea?"

"Well, we still want to make a car," said Sam. "But we came up with the idea of using lighter materials and making a bunch of small model cars. That way, we

could power them with balloons and race them."

"What do you think?" Maddie asked Bella.

Bella hesitated. Balloon-powered cars couldn't do nearly as many cool things as computer-powered cars. But racing sounded fun, and they had to start somewhere!

"Sounds great," she told her friends. "Let's go look for materials!"

After a trip to Bella's kitchen recycling bin and a spin through the craft supply containers in the club-house, the friends had assembled lots of good items for their project: plastic bottles and wood scraps for

the car frames, plus bottle tops, jar lids, and big buttons from Maddie's stash of sewing supplies for wheels. They also collected all sorts of decorations, paints, and fasteners.

While Bella was organizing everything into neat piles, Sam came over to her.

"Are you really not going to join the robotics team?" he asked. "That sounds like your dream team!"

Bella shrugged. "All the kids were older than me. And they've probably

all built tons of robots before," she said.

"Bet they haven't starred in a rock band or tie-dyed a shirt for the mayor," Sam said with a wink.

Bella laughed. Maybe Sam was right. Maybe she was psyching *her-self* out. Maybe . . . she'd give the robotics team another shot.

CHAPTER
5

Hold That Thought

And Bella did give it another shot. The following week, she was back in Mrs. Jacobs's classroom.

"Glad you came back," said Mrs. Jacobs with a smile.

Bella smiled, but she wondered if Mrs. Jacobs would be the *only* one who was happy to see her.

This time Bella had made a point

of getting there early and finding a good seat. As the older kids arrived, though, she couldn't help but notice that none of them said hello or sat down near her.

"Okay, let's get started," said Mrs. Jacobs. "So, the contest challenge has been announced and it is a 'green' one. This means our robot will need to do two things to help the environment. Why don't we start by brainstorming ideas?"

Bella may have been obsessed with all things computer and electronics, but she also definitely cared about the environment. She raised her hand.

Mrs. Jacobs asked the robotics team captains to run the brainstorming session. Naomi called on people to share their ideas, and Bryce wrote the ideas down on the board.

"Let's see," said Naomi, looking around the room. "Kimaya?"

"Our robot could monitor sunlight and move plants in response, so they get the optimum amount of sunlight."

"Great idea," said Naomi. Bella waved her hand, but Naomi called on a boy named Angelo instead.

"Maybe our robot could run on solar power?" he suggested.

"Very cool," said Naomi.

Finally, Naomi pointed at Bella.

"Me?" asked Bella, feeling a little self-conscious. "My name is Bella. You guys have a lot of great ideas. I have one to add, which is that our robot could—"

RIIIIIIINNNNGGGG!

At the sound of the bell, everyone

jumped up and grabbed their things. Everyone except Bella, who just sat there in disbelief.

Mrs. Jacobs came over and put a hand on her shoulder. "I'll bet you had a good idea. Can you hang on to it for next time?"

Bella nodded, but she wasn't sure. The older kids probably wouldn't even like her idea. Plus, they had so many good ideas of their own, they didn't need a little *kid*'s help.

Almost as if she had read Bella's mind, Mrs. Jacobs added, "'Though she be but little, she is fierce.'"

Bella looked up, confused.

"It's from Shakespeare," explained Mrs. Jacobs. "It's my way of saying that you matter. So, don't doubt yourself, okay?" She winked at Bella.

"Okay," said Bella. But she didn't wink back.

CHAPTER
6

Bella Breaks Down

After school, Bella and her mom went to the supermarket. Bella's mom did the grocery shopping, but she left the cooking up to Bella's dad, who was a chef.

In the produce aisle, Mrs. Diaz suggested, "Why don't you get the fruits and I'll get the veggies."

"Okay," said Bella. She selected

a pineapple, a bunch of bananas, and a bag of apples. Then she saw that mangoes were on sale. But as Bella took a mango from the display pile . . .

THUMP! SPLAT!

Several mangoes rolled off and landed on the floor. One was overripe and burst when it hit the ground, splattering Bella and other shoppers with sticky juice.

“I’m so sorry!” Bella bent down to pick up the mangoes. As she did, she dropped everything else she was trying to balance: the pine-apple, the bananas, and the bag of apples. The fruit went flying in different directions.

"Are you okay, sweetie?" asked a store employee, coming over to help.

Bella nodded. The employee was just trying to be nice, but he made Bella feel like a helpless little kid.

Just then Bella's mom appeared, holding a bunch of kale.

"Bella, *que pasó*? What happened?" she asked.

"I . . . I was just getting some mangoes, but then everything fell. . . ." Bella felt so frustrated. She couldn't do anything right, and now here she was about to bawl like a baby in the middle of the produce aisle!

Her mom helped her collect everything. "There we go!" she announced once all the fruit was in the shopping cart.

"What's wrong, Bella?" asked her mom after they moved on to the bread aisle. "You're so quiet today."

Bella shrugged, but said nothing.

They passed a shopping cart with a little boy in the seat. Bella's mother smiled at him, then turned to Bella. "I don't remember you ever sitting still in the cart. You just wanted to *push* the cart. You used to pretend it was a race car, remember?"

Bella smiled at the memory. But then it made her think of building the race cars, which made her think of Sam's suggestion about the robotics team, which made her think about that team meeting again. And that memory *didn't* make her smile.

"It's just hard sometimes," she told her mom. "I'm too big for little kid stuff, but I'm too little for anyone to take me seriously." And the next thing Bella knew, it all came tumbling out: the flyers, the robotics team meeting, everything.

"I should probably just quit," she told her mom. "I mean, it's not like they're going to let me do anything—they didn't even want to hear my ideas! And they don't need a *little kid* messing things up. I mean, you saw what happened with the fruit. I'd probably drop their robot or break it—"

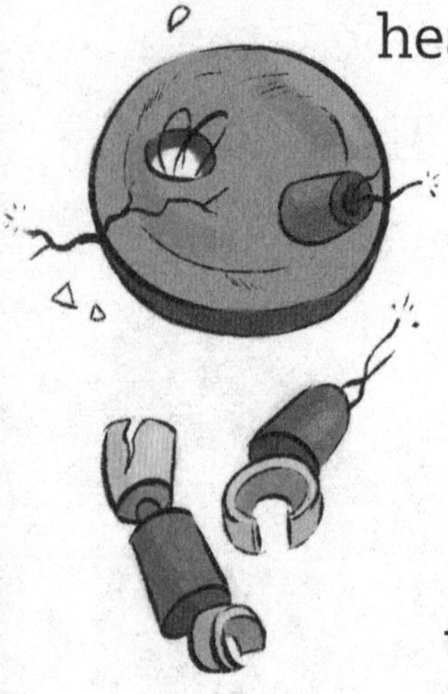

Bella's mom cut her off. "Do you know how your father got his big break?" she asked.

"No," said Bella. "How?"

“Well, he was in culinary school, and every student was required to prepare the same dish for a famous chef. Your father read the

instructions again and again, but something didn't look right to him. The recipe called for a *tablespoon* of salt, and your dad was pretty sure this would be overpowering. Finally, he trusted his intuition and made the adjustment—to a *teaspoon* of salt—and turned in his dish."

"What happened?" asked Bella.

"The famous chef went down the line of dishes like this." Bella's mom pretended to take a spoonful of soup, then made a pained face.

"Again and again, until he came to your father's dish."

Bella's mom took another pretend sip. This time, she beamed happily. "That famous chef offered your father his very first job. And you know what he told your dad? 'Anyone can chop up ingredients. But a true artist uses his mind, not just his hands.'"

"That's true when it comes to programming, too," said Bella. She thought for a moment. She'd give the robotics team *one* more shot.

CHAPTER
7

The Dream Machine

That Saturday the craft clubhouse came to life—loudly—as all four friends sawed, sanded, painted, and decorated their race cars.

Emily, the master builder, was in charge of wheel alignment. She carefully inspected each car to ensure a smooth ride. When she finished, the friends lined up their cars to admire them.

Sam's was, of course, beautifully painted with bright swirls of color. He had named his Rainbow Racer.

Maddie's car was purple and paisley and had a sequined fabric racing skirt around the bottom. Hers was called the Fast and the Fabulous.

Emily's car was called Solid Gold since it was *definitely* solid and Emily had spray-painted nuts and bolts gold and applied them to her car.

Bella called her car the Dream Machine.

"What are all those doodads you've got on there?" asked Maddie.

"My Dream Machine doesn't have 'doodads,'" said Bella. "Those are sensors that can measure the amount of air left in its tank, plus compressed air and also a hose to reinflate it!"

Everyone was super impressed.

"I think it's race time!" Emily said excitedly.

The four friends carried their cars out to Bella's driveway. Using chalk, they marked a starting line, race track, and finish line. Maddie brought along a checkered starting flag she had made too.

With balloons inflated, they positioned the four cars next to one another. Together they chanted, “On your marks, get set . . . GO!”

Everyone let go of their balloons and jumped back.

Three cars blasted off.

But the Dream Machine sputtered. Then scooted. Then stopped only an inch from the starting line.

Bella picked it up while her friends chased after their speeding cars. She felt a rush of the same embarrassment.

If she couldn't make a simple balloon-powered car, how would she be able to make it on the robotics team?

CHAPTER
8

Less Is More

"I don't understand," said Bella, studying her car. The sensors were still in position. The refill tank was full, so maybe the sensor malfunctioned?

"Try it again," said Emily, who had returned with the others to the starting line. Bella inflated the balloon again, set the car in position, and . . . nothing.

"Ugh!" Bella kicked the Dream Machine in frustration. One of the sensors fell off, making things worse.

Maddie picked up Bella's car and the broken sensor and handed both to her friend. "Try it now?" she suggested.

"I just did!" said Bella.

"No. I mean try it now that a piece is missing," explained Maddie. "I didn't want to say anything before because your car *looked* so cool. But you know what they say: Sometimes less is more."

Bella raised an eyebrow. Maddie's usual rule, especially when it came to accessorizing, was: *more* is more. But Bella decided to give her car another try.

This time the car actually moved! Not very fast, but it was clear Maddie had a point. Without the additional weight, the car could actually roll.

"To the clubhouse!" yelled Bella.

"Don't you want to race again?" asked Sam.

Bella shook her head. "You guys go ahead. I've got to hop online and do some research first!"

Half an hour later, Bella rejoined her friends in the driveway.

"Whoa!" said Maddie when she saw Bella's car. The car had none of the "doodads" from before. No bells, no whistles, no compressed-air tank—nothing.

"I know what you're thinking," said Bella. "How can it be *my* car when it looks so low tech? But here's what I learned from my research. Race car designers don't just make cars sleek to look cool. They do it to minimize drag and wind resistance. They also select specific

wheel sizes for performance, and try to eliminate extraneous ergonomic impediments."

"Um, English, please?" said Sam.

Bella flipped her car over and showed them the underside. "See? I removed the extra tank to make it much lighter than before. And I

made the wheels bigger, so my car would roll faster and be less likely to skid."

"Well, let's test out your theory!" said Maddie excitedly.

Again the friends inflated their balloons and lined up their cars.

"On your marks, get set, GO!"

This time, all four cars shot forward, with one car taking a distinct lead over the others: the new-and-improved Dream Machine. Cheering, the four friends ran after them, all the way to the finish line.

Maybe I do have something to contribute to that robotics team after all, Bella thought happily.

CHAPTER
9

The Big Day Disaster

Week after week, Bella kept showing up for robotics meetings. The team's robot was looking really cool. Most of the time, Bella just did whatever the older kids instructed her to do. Occasionally she'd ask a question—she really did want to learn more about robotics, after all!

When the day of the competition

finally came, Bella's mom drove her to the town hall.

Bella took a deep breath and walked in. Throughout the halls there were lots of adults and older kids in team T-shirts yelling, cheering, and carrying half-assembled robots.

When Bella finally found the exhibit hall, she gasped at the sight of it. There were booths everywhere, each with a team of kids, a presentation explaining their project, and

a robot on a display table. There were robots rolling, robots climbing, robots printing out data results, and so many other cool projects.

"Bella! Over here!"

Bella turned. There was Mrs. Jacobs, wearing a bright green MASON CREEK ROBOTICS TEAM T-shirt. The next thing she knew, Bella was wearing one too. It was big on her, but Bella was thrilled. Now she felt like she was officially part of the team!

There was just one problem: The *team* wasn't working very well as a team. Bryce was upset and Naomi was frantic. All the other kids were crowded around a smartphone, offering suggestions to a girl named Jenna. She was trying to get the robot to work, but she wasn't succeeding.

"Jenna! Shut it down and start over."

"Jenna, press one-two-three at once. That will override the system."

"Just turn it off. Not the phone, the bot. You need to reboot it."

Meanwhile, the robot seemed to be trying to respond to several commands at once. They had programmed it to move until it detected light on its solar panels. Then it was supposed to go retrieve a potted plant, bring it to the light source, and position it accordingly. Instead, it was rolling back and forth under the light source the team had set up. It kept knocking over potted plants. Dirt was spilling everywhere!

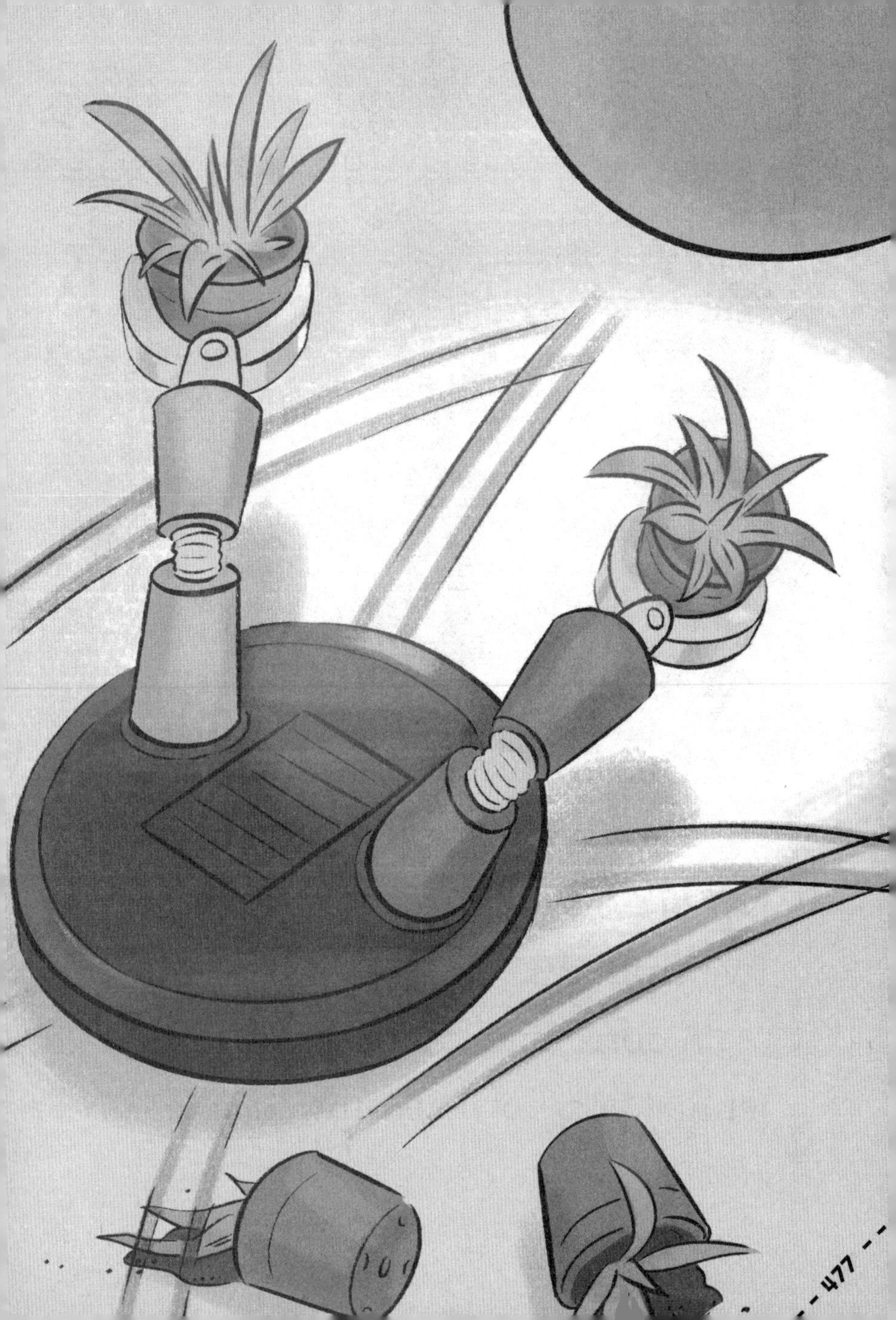

"This is a disaster," wailed Bryce.

"We have to get it together!" said Naomi. "We are up for judging in five minutes."

"I don't know what to do," said Jenna. "It's not listening to me!"

Just then Bella had a thought.

"Um . . . could I try something?" she asked Jenna.

Jenna looked up from the screen, startled. But she seemed to realize that she wasn't going to be able to get the robot to work. She handed the phone to Bella.

“Thanks,” said Bella. She pulled up the string of commands on the phone and quickly began to edit it. When she was finished, she handed the phone back to Jenna. She swept the dirt off the display table and put the plant into the robot’s arms.

“Try it now,” she told Jenna.

Jenna did as she was told . . . and so did the robot.

“Woo-hoo!” All the team members began to cheer as the robot

started moving toward the light source, then rotated the plant into position.

Just then the judges arrived at their booth. Bella thought they looked impressed as they took notes.

As soon as the judges had moved on, all eyes turned to Bella.

"How did you get it to work?" asked Naomi.

Bella smiled and showed her teammates the string of commands.

"I realized that we had added several unnecessary steps to the equation. It occurred to me that we might be more successful if we cut them out and streamlined it. Sometimes less is more," she added.

"Nice work," said Naomi with a genuine smile.

Now hopefully *less* would be *more* to the judges, who were already totaling everyone's scores.

CHAPTER 10

Dreams Come True

"Are we too late?" asked Sam, running up to Bella. Maddie, Emily, and Bella's parents followed seconds later.

"Nope," said Bella. "Check it out."

She borrowed the phone controller from Jenna and put the robot into action. Once again, it performed perfectly.

“That is so cool!” said Emily.

Bella smiled. Now *this* was a dream machine.

A crowd was gathering around the judging stand. The judges had posted the results!

Naomi ran over, and Bella and

the rest of the team waited with bated breath.

When Naomi ran back, Bella burst out, “So? How did we do?!”

Naomi smiled. “Our team won the silver cup—we got second place overall!”

The Mason Creek Robotics Team jumped up and down and cheered.

Then Naomi turned to Bella. "Bella, I'm sorry for the way I treated you when you first joined the team."

"So am I," added Bryce. "We should have given you more of a chance from the start. After all, if it hadn't been for you, we would have finished in last place—not second!"

"Thanks, guys. Although I wish we had come in first," Bella admitted.

Naomi laughed. "Well, we came

Creek
Team
Mason
Robotics

in fifth last year, so this is a big win for us! And next year maybe we *will* come in first. You're staying on the team, right?"

Bella raised her eyebrows. "Well, yeah, I guess," she said, both surprised and flattered. "I actually have an idea that might be fun to try out. Have you guys ever programmed a race car?"

Naomi and Bryce's eyes got wide. "A race car robot?! That sounds awesome!" said Naomi.

Bella smiled. She was really happy she hadn't given up on the robotics team—or on her Dream Machine. As it turned out, sometimes you just had to work a little harder for your dreams!

How to Make . . .

A Balloon-Powered Race Car

What you need:

Balloon
Flexible straws (3)
Tape
Water bottle
Bottle caps (4)
Sponge
Scissors
Barbecue skewers or chopsticks (2)

Make the jet by putting the long end of a flexible straw into the balloon.

Use tape to secure the straw and the balloon and to make sure no air will escape.

Step 3:

Lay the water bottle down. With scissors, poke two holes in the bottle. The holes should be directly across from each other on the part of the bottle that will be the back of the car.

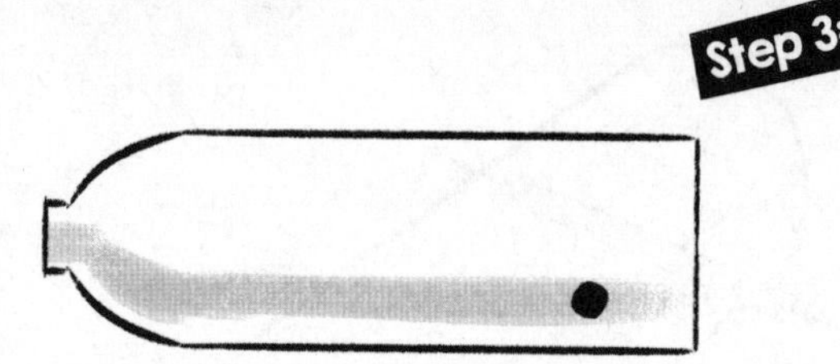

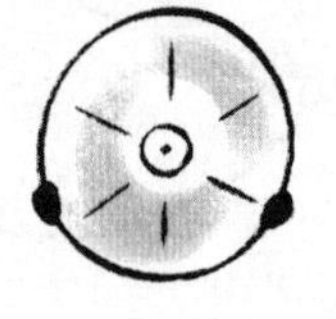

Step 4:

Slide a straw through the two holes. This is the axle. Adjust the axle so it goes straight across.

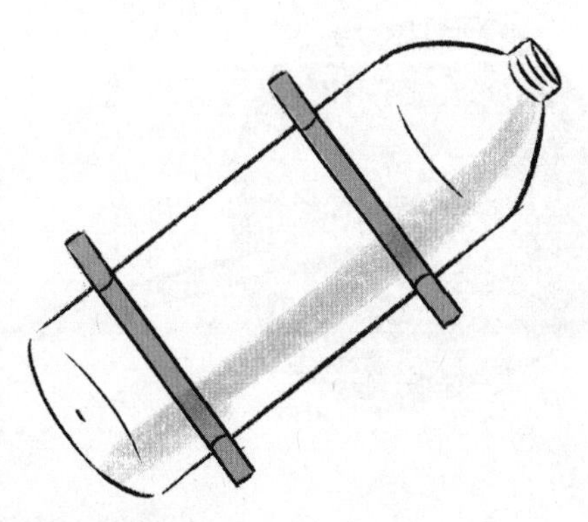

Repeat steps 3 and 4 at the top of the bottle, which will be the front of the car.

Slide a barbecue skewer through each straw.

Cut your sponge into squares that will fit into the bottle caps. Then wedge a square of sponge into each bottle cap to make the wheels.

Use a spare skewer to poke holes into the center of each sponge.

Push the sponge side of each wheel onto the ends of the skewers coming from the straws.

Use scissors to poke two more holes. One toward the top of the bottle, and one on the bottom of the bottle.

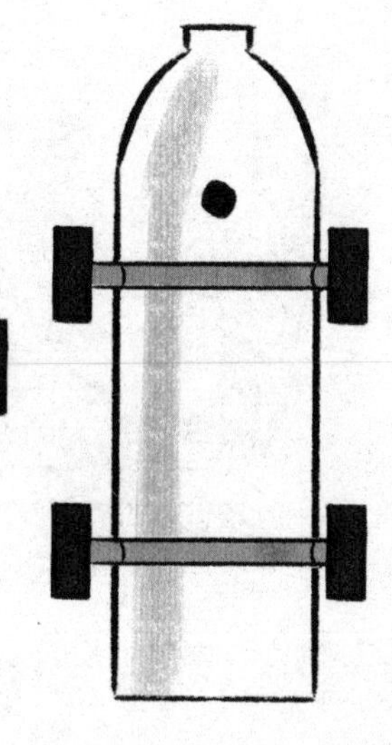

Step 11: Push the jet into place so that the straw's balloon end pokes out the hole toward the top and the open end pokes out the bottom.

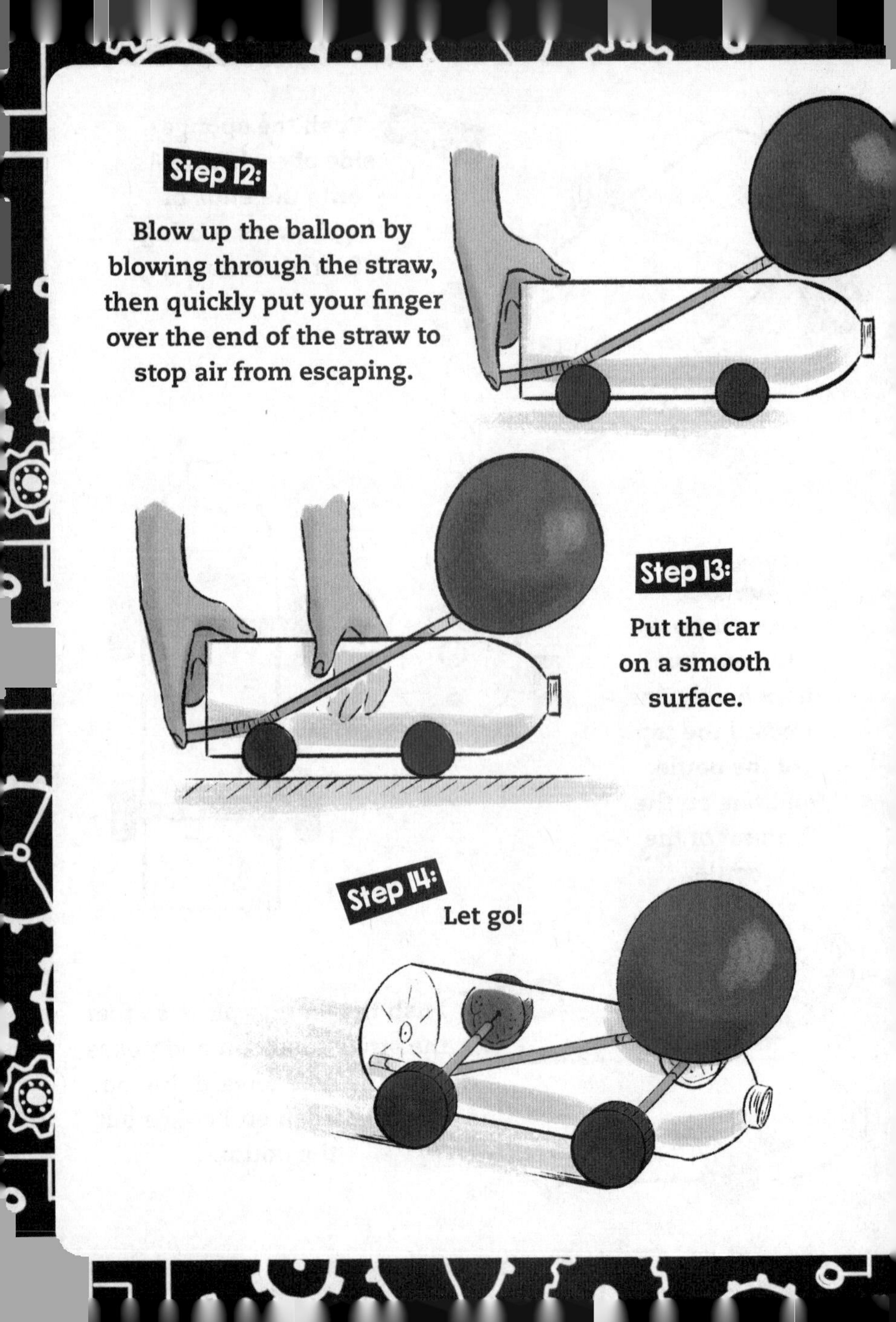
Step 12:
Blow up the balloon by blowing through the straw, then quickly put your finger over the end of the straw to stop air from escaping.
Step 13:
Put the car on a smooth surface.
Step 14:
Let go!

Here's a sneak peek at the next Craftily Ever After book!
Craftily Ever After
#5
DIY Pet Shop
by Martha Maker
illustrated by Xindi Yan

CHAPTER
1

Knot a Problem

Bella Diaz was in the craft clubhouse—formerly known as the old shack in her backyard—waiting for her three best friends to arrive. It was Saturday afternoon. As often as possible, and especially on weekends, the foursome met up at the clubhouse to do craft projects together.

Knock, knock-knock, knock!

Bella jumped to her feet at the sound of the familiar knock. But when she opened the door, she did not see a familiar face. All she could see were sequined sneakers, bright purple leggings, and two hands carrying a towering pile of fabric pieces.

"Maddie?" Bella guessed.

"How'd you know?" The sneakers shuffled forward, and the giant pile of material landed with a soft *thump* on the big worktable. Maddie Wilson's trademark grin came into view.

"Lucky guess," said Bella, smiling back. Maddie was the stylish seamstress of the bunch, and since her mother was a fashion designer, she often got her mom's leftover scraps.

"Very cool," Bella added. "But what are all these scraps for?"

"My mom just finished creating an entire line of fleece jackets, so she gave me the leftover material. It's so cuddly and soft. I thought we could make knotted blankets."

"What's a knotted blanket?" asked Emily Adams as she and Sam Sharma entered the clubhouse. Now all four friends were there.

"This!" Maddie showed them a pattern. "See? You cut out a square at each corner, and then you cut fringe all the way around. After that you line up the two pieces of cloth and knot the fringe together. Or braid them, if you prefer. There are lots of ways to do it."

The four friends were game, so they each selected fabric pieces and quickly got to work.

Or tried to.

"This is harder than it looks," said Emily.

Sam nodded. "My knots are *not* holding."

Bella came over to take a look. "Do either of you know how to make a square knot?"

They didn't, but they learned quickly when Bella showed them a how-to video on her computer. "See? *Knot* a problem," she joked.

Everyone laughed.

Before long, all four friends were working away, knotting and braiding the fringes on their blankets in different patterns.

“These are cool,” said Sam. “What are we going to do with them when we’re done?”

“I’m not sure,” admitted Maddie. “They’re pretty small. I guess we could leave an opening and put stuffing between the two layers? That would make them into pillows.”

“They’d make cute dog beds, too,” said Emily.

“Ohh, that reminds me . . . ,” said Sam. “It’s my turn to take Bibi out. If I’m late, it will be trouble.”

“Sam, you are so lucky,” said Emily. “I wish I could have a dog, but my parents think it’s too much work.”

“Well, they’re kind of right,” said Sam.

"Hey, whose side are you on?" said Emily, jabbing Sam's arm playfully.

"I'm just saying, it's totally worth it, but it *is* a lot of responsibility and a lot of work," Sam said with a smile.

Emily nodded, but the only part she heard loud and clear was: "totally worth it."

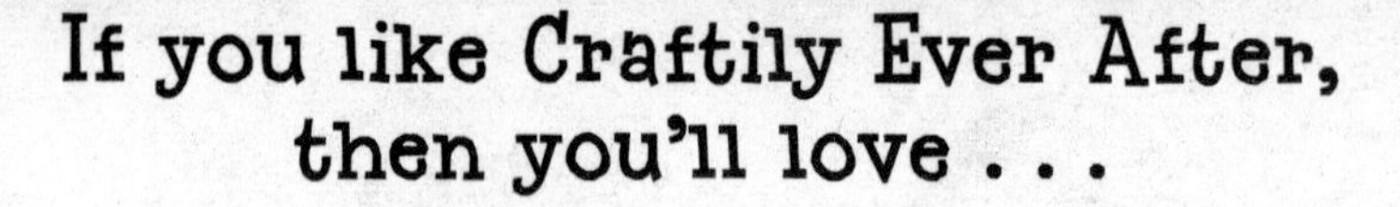
If you like Craftily Ever After,
then you'll love . . .

the CRITTER club
Missing Puppy
All About Ellie
Liz Learns a Lesson
Marion Takes a Break
EBOOK EDITIONS ALSO AVAILABLE
from LITTLE SIMON
simonandschuster.com/kids